THE
King's Swift Rider

BOOKS BY
MOLLIE HUNTER

Cat, Herself

Day of the Unicorn

A Furl of Fairy Wind

Gilly Martin the Fox

The Haunted Mountain

Hold On to Love

The Kelpie's Pearls

The Knight of the Golden Plain

The Mermaid Summer

The Pied Piper Syndrome

A Sound of Chariots

A Stranger Came Ashore

The Stronghold

Talent Is Not Enough

The Third Eye

The Thirteenth Member

The Three-Day Enchantment

Thomas and the Warlock

The Walking Stones

The Wicked One

You Never Knew Her As I Did!

THE King's Swift Rider

A NOVEL ON ROBERT THE BRUCE

Mollie Hunter

HARPERCOLLINSPUBLISHERS

J

Library of Congress Cataloging-in-Publication Data
Hunter, Mollie, date
    The king's swift rider : a novel on Robert the Bruce / Mollie Hunter.
        p.   cm.
    Summary: Unwilling to fight but feeling a sense of duty, sixteen-year-old Martin joins
Scotland's rebel army as a swift rider and master of espionage for its leader, Robert the Bruce.
    ISBN 0-06-027186-8
    1. Robert I, King of Scots, 1274–1329—Juvenile fiction. 2. Scotland—History—Robert I,
1306–1329—Juvenile fiction. [1. Robert I, King of Scots, 1274–1329—Fiction. 2. Scotland—
History—Robert I, 1306–1329—Fiction.] I. Title.
PZ7.H9176Ki 1998   98-10633
[Fic]—dc21   CIP
                                                                                    AC

Typography by Becky James
2   3   4   5   6   7   8   9   10
❖
First Edition

To H—a life

Contents

AUTHOR'S NOTE xiii

PART I
The Lion As Prey 1

PART II
The Lion As Hunter 83

PART III
The Lion Rampant 151

Epilogue 233

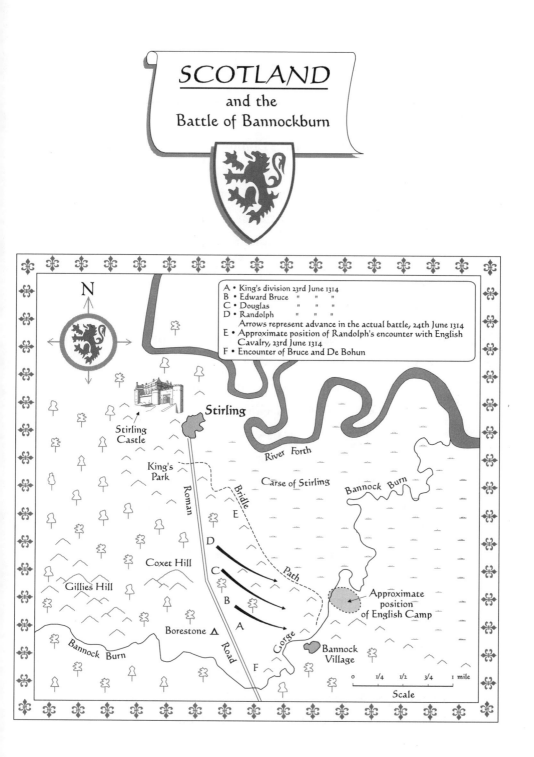

SCOTLAND
and the
Battle of Bannockburn

A • King's division 23rd June 1314
B • Edward Bruce   "   "   "
C • Douglas   "   "   "
D • Randolph   "   "   "
Arrows represent advance in the actual battle, 24th June 1314
E • Approximate position of Randolph's encounter with English Cavalry, 23rd June 1314
F • Encounter of Bruce and De Bohun

N

Stirling Castle

Stirling

King's Park

River Forth

Carse of Stirling

Bannock Burn

Coxet Hill

Gillies Hill

Borestone △

Roman

Bridle

Path

Road

Gorge

E

D

C

B

A

F

Approximate position of English Camp

Bannock Village

Bannock Burn

0   1/4   1/2   3/4   1 mile

Scale

Dramatis Personae

ANSELM, Brother Anselm, Dominican friar and the king's
    master of espionage

BINNOCK, William, farmer near town of Linlithgow

BOHUN, Sir Henry de, English cavalry leader

BOYD, Sir Robert, officer in Bruce army

BRECHIN, Sir David, leader of Buchan army

BRUCE, Robert, Earl of Carrick and King of Scots

BRUCE, the lord Edward, brother to the king

COMYN, John, Earl of Buchan, mortal enemy of the Bruce

CRAWFORD, Catriona, a widow

        Martin, her younger son

        Morag, her elder daughter

        Sean, her elder son

        Shona, her younger daughter

DALGLEISH, Andrew, soldier in Bruce army

DOUGLAS, James, the "Black," officer in Bruce army

EDWARD I, King of England

EDWARD II (son of Edward I), King of England

EWEN, a gillie (servant lad)

FARQUHAR, Alec, soldier in Bruce army

FRANCIS, William, ex-member of garrison, Edinburgh
    Castle

GAVESTON, Piers, courtier to Edward II

IRWIN, Sir William de, standard-bearer to the Bruce

KEITH, Sir Robert, Marischal of Scotland

LENNOX, Malcolm, Earl of Lennox, officer in Bruce army

LORN, John of, leader of MacDougal army

MACDOUGAL, name of clan in northwest Scotland

MACDOWELL, name of clan in southwest Scotland

MARJORIE Princess, daughter of the Bruce

MARTIN, The king's swift rider (see under *Crawford*)

MORAG (see under *Crawford*)

MORAY, David, Bishop of Moray

MOUBRAY, Sir Philip, governor of Stirling Castle

PEMBROKE, Earl of, commander-in-chief, English forces
     in Scotland

PICARD, Jean-Marie de, French noble, squire to the Bruce

PILCHE, Alexander, Sheriff of Inverness

RANDOLPH, Sir Thomas, nephew to the Bruce

ROBERTON, Hugh, soldier in Bruce army

ROSS, Earl of, pro-English ruler of province of Moray

SEAN, soldier in Bruce army (see under *Crawford*)

SHONA (see under *Crawford*)

SIM OF THE LEAD HOWES, lead miner & inventor of
     rope ladders

WALLACE, William, hero of first attempts to free Scotland

WALTER (Sir Walter of Ross), son of Earl of Ross

WISEMAN, Sir William, leader of Moray men supporting
     the Bruce

Author's Note

It was the death of Scotland's king in 1292 that led to the events in this story. With civil war threatening between the main claimants to the throne, King Edward of England was called in to arbitrate between them.

One of these, John Balliol, Lord of Galloway, was backed by the Earl of Buchan, head of the powerful Comyn family. The other was Robert Bruce, grandfather of the Bruce of this story. King Edward chose Balliol, a weak man through whom he meant to rule Scotland, and it was when Balliol at last rebelled against being treated as a mere puppet king that Edward seized the opportunity to do so.

In a campaign of unparalleled ferocity he destroyed Balliol, garrisoned Scotland with his troops, and declared himself its king. But such was the brutality of his rule that it led eventually to a general uprising led by that legendary hero William Wallace; and among the nobility who rallied to him were Robert Bruce, Earl of Carrick and also grandson of the Bruce who had opposed Balliol's claim to the throne, together with John "the Red," leader of the Comyn faction. Yet bravely as the rebels fought, Wallace was still eventually defeated, dragged to London, and executed.

The only man who dared then to continue the struggle was the Bruce who had fought with Wallace and who, by then, had inherited his grandfather's claim to the throne. But to establish that claim, he had first to reach agreement with the Red Comyn. His attempt to do so ended in a quarrel that led to the Comyn's death—thereby putting Bruce at blood feud with the whole of that powerful family, and so also leaving him with but one option. He could leave Scotland to its fate, or else he could have himself crowned King of Scots and fight on, as such, against the combined might of Edward and the house of Comyn.

Bruce chose to fight, and his story from that point is told here as accurately as research will allow. But in oral tradition there is much also of his epic struggle to free Scotland, and it is from this source that the character of the king's swift rider has been evolved.

PART I

The Lion As Prey

Chapter One

For hours, that day, I had watched the hunted man.

I had a vantage point in this—the ridge of hill where I had got the two hares meant for my family's dinner. The clearness of the March air also allowed me to scan far and wide across the moor beneath, and when I first saw him, the man had been in the lead of around sixty others, all briskly marching. Then from somewhere in the distance behind his band had come the sound of hunting-horns.

The man swung round to his followers with gestures that sent them scattering in all directions—his intention in this, I guessed, being to increase each one's chance of escape. The moor became dotted with running figures, vanishing some-times into its broken landscape, suddenly reappearing to run again. The horn calls, meanwhile, were growing rapidly louder, with yelling voices now sounding through them.

I brought my gaze back to the man who had led the

fugitives. He was running in my direction, with only one other now alongside him. He halted—very suddenly. I looked to my left and saw what he had seen—five men running fast, but with swords drawn, and coming towards him at an angle that would intercept his path of flight.

The man's sole companion had halted also at sight of the attackers, and would immediately have turned to run from them if the man himself had not checked him in this and then stood firm, his own sword unsheathed for action. Readily then, the other took example from him. The five came on, yelling menace, and closed in battle. Steel flashed in the spring sun, flashed and flashed again.

I heard the repeated ring of blade striking blade, saw what seemed to my untrained eye to be no more than a meaningless movement of figures dodging, weaving, and staggering over the uneven ground of the moor. And then out of all this, my view became that of a veritable net of steel whirling around the man's head—because now he was fighting alone, his companion disarmed, sword arm drooping, the other arm clutched across his chest. But three of the five were also out of the fight by then, all of them lying prone on the heather of the moor. And it was this lone man who was pressing home the attack against the other two!

I have since then seen much fighting, but never anything to outdo the controlled fury of that man's swordplay. One of his remaining antagonists went down. Faintly I heard the howl of fear the other gave as he realized he now stood alone against that terrible sword. And then, even as he fell before it,

I saw distantly a wave of the pursuers, some afoot, some on horseback.

The man ducked for cover behind one of the great rock masses that littered the moor, dragging his wounded companion with him. From there, he got them both as far as a clump of small birch trees, and from there again into the further concealment of a great stretch of prickly whin bushes. The pursuers, meanwhile—lacking the viewpoint that showed me how their quarry was using the broken terrain of the moor to such advantage—were searching it more or less at random. And only after my attention had been for a while diverted to them did I realize that their quarry had vanished from my sight also.

For an hour and more, I watched their search—a fruitless one, since all they found were the bodies lying where the fight of two against five had taken place. They gathered in a group around these. And then, through the sound of their curses, I heard distantly that of another and infinitely more dangerous pursuit—the baying of a bloodhound. And as if this had been a signal they had all been waiting for, the pursuers instantly abandoned their search to turn and race towards it.

The moor lay apparently deserted, then, of all life, and silent except for that distantly heard baying. I waited, my eyes traveling back and forth over the still landscape, my blood chilling as the hound's call drew nearer, grew louder. No one, it seemed to me, however criminal he was, deserved to be so hunted! But this was Scotland, of course, in the year of Our Lord thirteen hundred and seven, and the English forces we had fought against so bitterly for ten years had the whole country in their grip. A grip so brutal, too, that they were merciless against anyone who dared stand against them.

To justify such a pursuit then, it must be that the "crime" of this man—so evidently the leader of those others I had first seen—must indeed have been to offer such opposition! Or so I concluded—and saw him at that moment newly emerged from the pile of heather and dead bracken that had enabled him and his companion to merge totally with their surroundings. Both stood for a moment with their heads cocked to the sound of the bloodhound's baying. Then both began to run— but not in a straight course, and soon I realized the reason for this.

Lying under the heather of our moors there is always a thick layer of the peat we use as fuel for our fires. And because of the way this peat dries out in summer after each of our rain-soaked Scottish winters, it splits into the irregular clefts we call peat hags. These peat hags, too, can be deep as well as wide, with streams of water trickling through the deepest of them. And even though this is not the swiftly flowing water that cannot possibly carry a scent, the man's progress then showed his hope that these streams would be enough to delay the hound's pursuit by at least temporarily throwing it off his trail.

Racing ahead of his wounded companion, but always encouraging the other to follow his example and always aiming for the deepest of the peat hags, he leapt down into each one and waded along the foot of it before regaining dry land again on its opposite bank. Each time he did so, he drew nearer to the river running between the moor and the ridge of hill where I knelt, tensely watching. And wondering, too, how long he could use this device before the hound's handlers caught sight of him—because they had now also come into my field of vision!

It was quite uncanny, too, considering all that had already happened on that moor, the way that hound was zigzagging to follow the scent of one particular man. He had been the leader, after all, of around sixty men who had all scattered in different directions. Yet still it had unerringly chosen the direction *he* had taken. And now it had reached the place where lay the five killed in the sword fight.

I watched it nosing out from there each one of the places where the man and his companion had hidden from the human pursuers—steadily nosing, until the device of wading along the bottom of the peat hags began, from time to time, to give it check. But that could not last, I told myself. Sooner or later, the man would *have* to break from whatever cover any one of these might now be giving him.

The flush of anger at that thought made me all the more aware of the warmth of that day's sun beating on my back. That awareness, in turn, brought to my notice the fact that the same warmth was bringing out the stink of the hares lying beside me—the hares I had netted for the family's dinner— and a vague idea in my mind took positive shape.

The only way the hunted man could hope to throw the hound completely off his scent was by reaching the river at the foot of the hill. And running in direct line from where I knelt was the very peat hag that now sheltered the man!

I snatched up my hares and raced down the hill towards the river, slid down the steep bank on its near side, and scrambled up the equally steep bank that faced me. At the mouth of the peat hag I knelt and called out softly:

"Are you there—the man they are hunting? Can you hear me? If you can, come quickly to the river, and I will save you."

A moment's silence, and then from somewhere in the dimness of the peat hag's overhanging bank, there was movement. Eyes glared out at me. The movement became two figures inching towards the end of the peat hag, the nearer one helping the other along.

I splashed quickly back across the stream and got ready to gut one of my hares. From the stream's far side, an answering voice called:

"How can you save me?"

I looked towards the peat hag. The man—a great, big fellow, taller than any I had ever seen, and broad with it—had emerged from there, dragging his wounded companion with him. I had the hare slit open by then. I scattered some of the guts around the place where I stood, threw some of the rest along the bank running upstream from there, and told him:

"By turning the bloodhound away from you—leading it upriver, while you lose your trail in the downstream."

He understood immediately how I would do that. He knew as well as I did that there is no dog—whatever else it may be tracking—that can resist being diverted from that

8

by the scent of hare. Without a word in reply, he lifted his companion bodily and began wading downstream, carrying the other in his arms.

I began running upstream, scattering the rest of the first hare's guts as I went. Then I trailed the skin of this hare behind me for a while, before slitting open the second hare and using its guts to continue the diversion. I scattered the hare scent as widely as I could, also, the further to delay the hound catching up on me—and certainly long enough for the man to wade so far downstream that it would just not be possible for the beast to pick up his trail again.

But then, of course, they did catch up with me—the first I heard of them being the baying of the hound itself. Then came the voice of its handler yelling curses at the beast, and I caught enough of this yelling to understand at last how it had so persistently picked out from among so many the trail of the man they were hunting. It was his own dog—bred by him, fed by his own hand. And there is no dog, surely—whatever its breed—that cannot nose out the scent of its own master.

I had not time, however, to wonder how they had managed to get hold of it. The hound, dragging its handler along with it, was leaping up on me by then, and behind it came the whole body of the hunting party. As I had guessed, too, there were indeed soldiers from the English garrison among them. And so, of course, these soldiers beat me—and not just for losing them their quarry, but also on suspicion that I had deliberately diverted the hound from the man's track.

So cruel, indeed, was their beating that I stopped at last

my pretense of sniveling over it—crying, instead, in such good earnest that the hound's handler intervened.

"Ach, leave him alone, will you? Anyone with an eye in his head, after all, can see he's not much more than a half-wit— a big laddie like him, bawling and weeping now like he was a baby!"

I backed him up in this by bawling all the louder—something that the English soldiers immediately treated as a great joke. But at least then they did leave me alone. The hound itself, meanwhile, had been tearing at what was left of my hares. I had nothing now for the pot. What was more, I could not risk these men's suspicions falling on any of my family. And so, just in case any of them had thoughts of following me, I knew I would have to take a very roundabout way to home.

It was late that day, accordingly, when I did finally arrive there. My elder brother, Sean, began immediately to jeer at me for having nothing to show for my day's absence, and was checked in this by the oldest of the family, my sister, Morag. My little sister, Shona, looked sad for me, as she always does when Sean teases. My mother started in alarm at the sight of my bruised face. Choosing my words as carefully as I could, I told her:

"A man was being hunted. And I was there. That is why I am bruised and have nothing for the pot."

She looked from me to the others. "That is all he needs to say," she warned them. And even little Shona understood then that her reason for speaking so was to remind them that what they did not know could not be beaten out of them.

My mother has other qualities, however, apart from being a woman of sense. She is a good cook who can make much of little, and since Sean at least had managed to get something for the pot, we did not go hungry that night. But above all, my mother is a poet—the best of her time; and after we had eaten, she let us hear some of her love songs, softly playing as she did so on her *clarsach*, her little harp.

I should have slept as soundly then as I always did after hearing her sing these. Yet still I had nightmare after nightmare—beginning, I suppose, with thoughts of how it is said among us that the love songs of women poets have so much of power and beauty that the sound of them survives even beyond death. Because of this, too, it is also said a woman poet must always be buried facedown, or else her songs arising from the grave will too much disturb the hearts of those still living.

So it was, then, that visions of my mother lying facedown in some place that was cold and dark were what first haunted my sleep. Then came nightmares of the hunt I had witnessed, and in some of these it was I, Martin Crawford, who was running for my life. In others it was the man—the big man who had swung that other up into his arms as easily as Sean or I would have lifted a small child. But in these other nightmares the man was being caught and savaged by a whole pack of hounds.

And then, in the morning, I saw him again.

He came stumbling up the slope of hill leading to our house, big shoulders slumped with weariness, the chain mail he wore spattered with mud, his helmet under one arm, early sunlight bright on the tawny-gold hair of his bowed head. And he was alone. I called out in astonishment. He looked up, recognition dawning at the sight of me, and spoke in a voice hoarse with fatigue.

"You see—you did save me."

"But how—" I was still so bewildered I could scarcely get the words out. "How did you find your way here?"

He shrugged. "Chance—blind chance. This is the first house I have seen in miles."

"And your companion—the one who fought the five with you. Where is he?"

"Dead of his wounds." Grimly, the words came blurting out of him. "And he was more than a companion. He was the child I grew up with, the son of the woman who nursed me— my foster brother."

I stood staring at him, realizing fully at last why, at even further risk to his own life, he had tried to save that wounded one. But he was looking beyond me by then, to where my mother had emerged from the doorway of our house.

"I am Catriona Crawford, a widow." Quietly she spoke to him. "The boy here is my second son, Martin. And you, sir— who are you? What brings you here?"

The man straightened and met her gaze squarely. But still, instead of telling who he was, he said merely, "I am hunted. I seek shelter." He paused, as if waiting to see what effect this announcement might have, and then bluntly added, "Can you—will you—give that to me?"

My mother came forward to stand by me. "I can, and I will," she told him. "For the sake of one I have heard is daily being hunted, I will shelter *any* hunted man."

For a long moment then, the man stared at her before he asked, "And who is this you have heard is at such risk?"

"A king!" As prompt to speak as he had been slow, my mother answered him. "One who is called Bruce—Robert the Bruce."

The man let out a long, sighing breath of seeming relief. Then, with a squaring of his broad shoulders, he drew himself up to the full stretch of his great height. And in all due reverence I swear to God I have never seen such majesty in anyone as there in was in him when he followed this by telling her:

"And I am he. I am Robert the Bruce, King of Scots."

Chapter Two

It was *sleep he needed*, more than anything else, and it was during his sleep that I thought deeply about him.

Here he was, the man who had been the young Earl of Carrick at the start of the revolt against the occupation of our land. But still, like others of the nobility, he had not been too proud to serve under one who was no more than a country gentleman—William Wallace, the great, the heroic leader of that revolt.

But now Wallace was dead—captured and most cruelly put to death. Our ten years of resistance to the tyranny of that occupation were completely at an end. Or so, at least, King Edward of England had thought! But that was because he had reckoned without the hunted man lying stretched out now, exhausted by the ordeal just past. Reckoned without Robert the Bruce!

The Bruce, he seemed to have forgotten, had a just and legal claim to Scotland's throne—a throne that had long lain empty. With Wallace dead, Edward had counted on our country's being left not only kingless, but leaderless as well. What a rude shock he must have had, then, when the Bruce had emerged as the new leader. And how he must have fumed at this last great act of defiance—the crowning of Bruce as King of Scots!

I stared into the fire under the pot of food my mother had ready against his wakening, and in the red and gold of the flames there I seemed to see the blaze of glory that had followed his coronation—the crowds who had flocked to follow him, the battles fought, the victories won. And then?

And then, disaster—the battle of Methven that had seen his forces surprised and utterly routed, the youngest of his four brothers captured and hanged, others near and dear to him also captured, his wife, Queen Elizabeth, banished to a nunnery, while he himself had been left with no choice except that of months spent in running and hiding from the English. . . .

Yet even from that he had fought back—but only to see another two of his brothers killed. And so how long, with the few men he had now, could he go on fighting—especially after yesterday's hair's-breadth escape? Could *any* man, however brave he was, continue against such odds as he faced?

He ate heartily, when he woke, of the food set before him, then reached for the chain mail discarded while he slept. I hurried to help him on with this, but it was at Shona he looked, and to her he said kindly:

"You are about the same age, I think, as my own little daughter—my Marjorie."

Shona blushed at being paid such attention, then timidly asked, "And where is she now, Sire, your Marjorie?"

Sean, Morag, and I tried to avoid looking at one another. Shona, our mother had warned, poor tenderhearted little Shona, must not be told of the cruelties devised for those captured along with Queen Elizabeth. We had shuddered ourselves, after all, to hear of the young countess condemned to imprisonment in an iron cage hung outside the walls of Berwick Castle. And as for the fate of that child, the king's daughter . . .

He glanced to our mother, his eyebrows raised in a gesture that plainly asked, *Should I tell her?* And quietly, in answer to this, she said:

"We have thought it right, so far, to keep so harsh a truth from Shona. But now, Sire, if your child of less than eleven years must continue to endure the torture inflicted on her, it seems right that my child of the same age should no longer be protected from knowing the full horror of it."

The Bruce nodded, and in a voice that seemed to me to be held tightly in control, he told Shona, "The Princess Marjorie is a prisoner in the Tower of London—kept there inside the kind of cage used for wild animals. She is being supplied with just enough food to keep her alive, and just enough clothing to keep her from freezing. And also—all on the orders of Edward of England—everyone except the Tower's governor has been forbidden, on pain of death, to speak so much as a word to her."

Shona gasped, her face going whiter than white. The Bruce began buckling on his sword; and in a shaking voice as she watched him doing so, she asked:

"But she will be free someday, Sire, will she not? Your Marjorie—she *will* be free?"

The Bruce touched a hand to the hilt of his sword. "That," said he grimly, "I can promise you. Someday my daughter will be free again. Someday, when the whole of Scotland also will be free!"

I should have known, I told myself. *This man will never go back on the choice he has made. He will win his fight, or he will die!*

"But Sire!" My mother had begun speaking over my thought, her voice agitated. "The entire country is garrisoned with English troops, while rumor has it that, even here in your own earldom of Carrick, you have managed to raise only a few hundred men. And so how *can* you free Scotland?"

"I do not know, dame. Not just now, that is. Not so long as all I hold of my country is the ground I stand on. But . . ." The Bruce turned from her to look towards the open doorway, the afternoon sunlight falling on his face.

"But this," he continued, "I do know. Or this, at least, I do believe. That the longer I fight, the more our people will rally to me, until at last I lead a whole nation once more in arms."

The lit face turned back to my mother, and in a quickened and sharper tone came the final words, "And there is nothing, dame, that can withstand one man at the head of a nation!"

"Wait, Sire!" Quickly my mother intercepted the move he made then towards the door. "There is one thing more I can do for you. You need men, and I have two sons. They will go with you."

She was offering Sean and me to fight with Bruce. And yet her husband—our father!—had died of the wounds he got fighting alongside Wallace!

The thought went flashing through my mind even as Sean exclaimed with delight at her words. The Bruce shot a glance at him before looking back to my mother to ask:

"You are sure of this?"

A nod was all he got in reply, but her face was tight with determination. And still testing her, he said, "But you are a widow. And these sons, surely, are your mainstay."

"I have managed since I was widowed," she told him, "and my youngest was then only a newly born babe. I will manage again. Also, my husband fought with Wallace, and so I know that this is what he, too, would have wished."

The Bruce threw a further glance at Sean—one that now took keen note of his sturdy build, the strong set of his shoulders.

"You have a weapon?"

"I have." Eagerly Sean responded. "My father's spear—the very one he used with Wallace."

"And how old are you?"

"Almost eighteen, Sire. Which is old enough, is it not, for soldiering? Because I have heard that James Douglas—that daring gentleman they call 'the Black Douglas'—was not much older than that when *he* joined you."

"Ah, yes, the Douglas." With a nod of approval at the name, the king continued, "But young as he was then, he has since become one of my two principal captains. And so come with me now if you wish—if, that is, you are truly willing to try proving your courage as much as he has done."

Sean was off, almost before the last of these words had been spoken, dashing away to arm himself with our father's spear. Within moments, he was back again, the spear over his shoulder, his face beaming as he announced, "I am ready, Sire!"

"But I am not!" Unbidden, the words came blurting out of me. And then, in answer to the look the Bruce turned on me, I tried hastily to explain, "Because, Sire, I do not wish to fight—not in *any* army."

"You do not wish to fight?" The Bruce, gazing down at me from his great height, was studying my face as if seeing it for the first time. "And so what *do* you wish to do?"

"We are poor people," I told him, "yet still I have book learning—from Brother Stephen of the abbey at Crossraguel. I asked him to teach me because I have a hunger for knowledge—a great hunger. And for one such as I, the only way to rise high enough to gain that knowledge is to be accepted into some order of the church."

"So you are ambitious!" The Bruce, still staring at me, said thoughtfully, "But that is something I can well understand, because I, too, have an ambition. And shall I tell you what that is?"

I nodded, wondering to myself what greater ambition he

19

could have than to have become, as he was, a king. And with that gaze of his growing even more intent, he went on:

"My ambition is to fulfill my vow of leading a crusade to the Holy Land. Yet still before I can do so, I must carry out the duty God has laid on me—that of making our people once again a free nation. But my title, remember, is not 'King of Scotland.' I am Robert, King of Scots—because here in Scotland it is king and people *together* who make up what we have always called 'the community of the realm.' And the duty that has been laid on me is therefore the duty also of *all* my people!"

His gaze by this time seemed to be almost literally boring into my own. He towered so far above me, too, the words themselves rang out with such a sound of command, that I could do no more than stammer:

"But—but Sire . . . I understand, of course, that duty must always come before ambition. Indeed, I have always been taught so. But—it is not only that I do not want to fight. I am only sixteen. I do not know *how* to fight. And so what use could I be to you?"

Unexpectedly then, he smiled, a smile so open and friendly that I could hardly believe this was the man who had so over-awed me. And smiling still, he said:

"A great deal of use, I think. You can read and write—rare abilities for one in the field, and therefore also ones which mean you could rise high in service to me. But meantime, I am a king sadly in lack of the attendants a king should have. And so meantime, also, you could be my page."

To be named as his page—a king's page! Into my mind

flashed all the stories I had heard about his coronation day, when the old, forbidden flag of Scotland—the scarlet lion rearing within its encircling band of scarlet lilies—had at last been triumphantly unfurled before all the great men who had gathered to see this happen. And he was offering me the chance to become, one day, a member of just such a company!

"Besides which"—the king's voice broke into that fleeting recollection—"the trick you played with the hares, the trick that saved my life—that showed your quickness of wit. And so you can see for yourself, can you not, that quick thinking can sometimes be of even greater use to me than simple willingness to fight?"

I glanced at the others. I had said nothing to them of my trick with the hares. And Sean, in particular, was looking back at me now with something more than wonder in his face. Sean, who had always thought himself so superior to me—was he perhaps also feeling envy at the prospect that had been held out to me? I would be even with him now, if that was so. Much greater in fact someday, if I did indeed rise high in service to the king! And yet . . .

It was still Sean who had always been the family's real provider. And so what about our mother and Morag, and Shona, if they were to be left now without even me to fend for them? I stood in speechless indecision, looking from one to another of them. And it was then, as if she had read this last of my thoughts, that my mother told me:

"You heard me, Martin. I managed before when you were still only a little boy of five. I will manage again."

"And I will see that she does," chimed in Morag, "because I can hunt and trap as well as any man. I can steer a plow too, as well as you or Sean ever did. And so, Martin, have no worries at all about us."

"Shona?" I turned lastly to Shona—timid little Shona who had always relied on me to protect her from all the fears she could so easily imagine. But rather than being afraid for herself, I found then, it was only the fate of that other child—the one held captive in London Tower—that was troubling her.

"And how can the king ever manage to set that little princess free," she asked, "if he does not get all the help he will need to free Scotland?"

There was no answer, I realized, to the reproach in *that* kind of argument! With the feeling that everything had conspired to overturn my first resistance to joining the king's army, I moved with Sean to take each of our family in a last embrace. And then, reaching for the only useful things I had—my hunting knife, my bow, and my quiverful of arrows—I followed as he and the Bruce went off to war.

We would be heading, Sean and I learned then, to the hiding place the Bruce had found for his men—the wild mountain valley of Glen Trool. Our direction would be by way of the house where he had first intended to take refuge from the hunt, because that was where he had told some of his men to meet again with him, and it could be that they were still expecting him there.

We had already heard, as it happened, that the owner

of that house and his two sons were thought to be friendly towards the Bruce. Also, since Sean knew better than I did the quickest route to their place from our own, it was he who then took the lead.

I followed the Bruce striding easily along behind Sean and soon became keenly aware of the obvious target he made. His height, the glint of gold from his hair and beard—there was no secret watcher who could fail to identify him. It would take nearly two hours, also, to reach the house in question—and these were hard times, when loyalty to a seemingly hopeless cause might well be outweighed by a bribe of English gold!

We reached our goal at last, however, without incident— a farmhouse of the better sort, with shrubbery lining the drive that led up to it, and a cluster of outbuildings to one side of the main building. But the Bruce, it seemed, could have been sharing some of my own misgivings on our way there. Or perhaps he was simply thinking then, as I was, that the place was too quiet. Much too quiet.

There was no sign of life around the house, no smoke from the chimney, no open door, no barking dog running to greet us. And halting our advance to let him survey this scene, he commanded Sean:

"Make your way roundabout to these outbuildings to see what they may hide. And Martin, you wait here with me."

Sean began casting round in a wide circle towards the outbuildings, keeping low all the time he did so. The Bruce and I waited, myself with gaze on Sean's progress, but the Bruce with his head constantly turning to keep as much as possible

23

in view of all approaches to us. And it was as well that he did so, because it was not from the outbuildings or from the house itself that surprise was sprung on us. That came from behind, with three men suddenly emerging from among the bushes where they had apparently hidden to watch our approach.

They were two young men and one much older—the owner of the house and his sons. The father had a sword at the ready. One of the sons held a battle-axe, and also had a sword at his side. The other son was advancing a spear, and he, too, had a sword. I was all ready to turn then and run, because even though I had already witnessed the Bruce conquer in a fight of one against three, I could see no hope at all of him doing so again. Not with three so variously armed as these! Yet this time too, instead of running, he held steady as rock, and calmly instructed me:

"If I am killed, you must instantly seek out the Black Douglas and tell him that he is the one I trust to avenge my death."

At the same time as he was saying this he was taking my bow from me and fitting to it an arrow from the quiver on my back. And while I was still wondering how and where I would find the Douglas, he had the bow strung and was facing towards the three attackers.

"So you have indeed sold me!" he shouted. "Sold me for English gold, you traitors!"

All three hesitated for a moment in face of this shouted challenge. Then the oldest of the three, the father, came on at a run. The Bruce had the bow drawn tight—and he was, I had heard, an expert archer. He fired the arrow. It took the man right in the middle of one eye, and he fell—killed instantly. The Bruce drew his sword.

The son armed with the battle-axe followed on his father's rush, swung at the Bruce, missed his stroke, stumbled, and was cut down with a single sweep of the king's great sword. The second son came on, spear outthrust before him. The Bruce sword whistled through the air in yet another sweep— but it was not at the man himself that he aimed. It was at the spear. And such was the force of *that* blow that the spear's blade was sheared clean off its shaft. Its owner gawped at the now-useless weapon, dropped it, and groped for his sword. The Bruce was swinging for another stroke. It fell before the groping hand had the sword halfway out of its sheath—and the third man then also lay dead.

I watched in such a daze that the wild sounds I heard as the third man fell seemed to me to be somehow the sounds evoked by the battle itself. The Bruce leant on his sword to look down at the corpse of this third man, and it was in that moment that I realized the source of the sounds I had heard.

There was a band of horsemen sweeping out from behind the outbuildings. They thundered towards us—a band of riders some twenty strong, all of them waving weapons, all ferociously yelling. I felt my legs beginning to buckle. They gave way completely, and despairingly as I sank to my knees, I thought:

So this is it! This is how I am to die!

Chapter Three

he Bruce stayed as he had been at the close of the attack, leaning on his sword and seemingly quite unconcerned by this new onslaught. The leading horseman drew the troop to a slithering halt a mere arm's length from him and was instantly out of the saddle.

"Sire!" His voice rising in joyous shout, he fell to his knees to seize the king's hand and kiss it. The others of the troop milled around the two of them, also loosing shouts of joy. I saw Sean among them, trying now to make his way back to the king. I saw, too, that the Bruce had begun raising their leader to his feet to embrace him as he would have embraced a younger brother.

I rose from my knees then, blushing for shame at having so mistaken the purpose of this troop. Their leader broke from the king's embrace, saying as he did so:

"We got word of the treachery that was planned, Sire, and rode as hard as we could to save you. But now, as it seems, you have saved yourself."

He paused there to look in wonder at the three dead men, and especially so at the one with the arrow through his eye. "But this man here," he exclaimed, "the one who is arrow shot. You had no such weapons when you were with the troop you ordered to scatter. And so how—"

"The boy, Douglas, the boy!" Interrupting, the Bruce pointed to me. "The bow and arrow were his."

"And pray, Sire—" Curiously the leader of the rescue party surveyed me. "Pray me, but who is he?"

"Martin Crawford, who is newly become my page," the Bruce told him.

I stared up at the man in front of me. He was young, a slim man of middling height, swarthy of face, black haired, black browed. And the king had named him "Douglas." So there he was in person now, the very man I had been told to find, the young hero whose coloring—not to mention his exploits against the English—had led to him being known as "the Black Douglas"!

"Welcome, Martin Crawford," he said, and smiled at me—a singularly pleasant smile, I thought, for one reputed to be so ruthless in battle. "Welcome to outlawry and the army of freedom!"

"Continue in command, Douglas!" The king's order rang out over this greeting. And so it was that we at last reached Glen Trool, two of the troopers mounted double so that the king could have a horse, Sean mounted behind another of the troopers, and myself riding crupper with fingers hooked into the belt around the lean waist of the Douglas.

It was dark by then, however, and I had no more than a confused impression of the camp there. But what I saw I did not like. The king's tent, where I was told I would henceforth sleep, was no more than a patched-together and untanned stretch of deerskins flung over the space between two tall rocks. For bedding there was only a pile of half-dry heather.

As for the men who had cheered his return there, never had I seen anything more like the ragged and desperate outlaws we called "broken men"—all of them, that is, except for one man who so much resembled the king that, even in my bewilderment then, I had no doubt that this was his one remaining brother, the lord Edward Bruce. And yet this was what the Black Douglas had called "the army of freedom."

The king himself, however, only shrugged when he saw my look of distaste for his so-called tent, and cheerfully informed me, "I was cradled in swansdown as a child, and in my grown years I slept between sheets of finest linen. But now I have become used to such hard lying. And so, in time, will you!"

And become used to it I did. In much shorter time than I had imagined, I became used altogether to my new kind of life. Not that I knew anything, of course, about the duties of a page. But I could at least keep bright the chain mail the king wore each time he led a band of the men in one of the swift attacks that, to the English troops patrolling the countryside, were a constant menace. I also foraged what I could in the way of food—ours being an army without supply lines—and cooked for him from the results of this forage.

It was not long, either, before I had made friends with the servant lads—the "gillies," as they were called—who looked after the horses. I found Sean, now much enjoying the weapons drill he was required every day to practice, and through him I began also to discover that the men of the army were not the kind of creature I had supposed them to be.

Far from that, in fact; they were just poor decent fellows stripped of all they possessed by the tyranny imposed on us, and with nothing left to sacrifice now except their lives. Some of them, too, were veterans of the Wallace campaign. But one and all, they were pinning their hopes on the Bruce as the only one who could now end that tyranny.

"And the king's brother?" I questioned them. "The lord Edward—what of him?"

"A brave soldier!" They were agreed on that. "Although, mind you"—cannily, it was volunteered then—"he can find it hard to accept the king's decision on the kind of hit-and-run tactics we must follow now."

"Because those are so far from the way a nobleman like him was trained to fight." That was Alec Farquhar, a Wallace veteran, now broadly grinning at me. "And because he is still a wee bit in love with memories of that."

"Which is not something you could say of the Black Douglas, nobly born as he is too."

The speaker this time was Hugh Roberton, a young fellow who had once been a farmer on the Douglas estates but now—like the Black Douglas himself—had lost everything to the English. There was much admiring talk then of the way he resembled the Bruce in the daring revenge he had taken for this, and of the ruthless fighting style that had since become his hallmark. But the other side of that coin—just as much for him as for the Bruce, they assured me—was his constant chivalry to the weak and helpless, with no woman or child ever having suffered at his hands.

"Says his prayers, too," they added, thus sealing for me this whole matter. Because one thing more I had by then added to my knowledge of the Bruce was that never a night passed without him kneeling to say his prayers.

Yet still, I wondered, what good would all that do him in the end—all that daring, that chivalry, that piety—when he had so small a force behind him?

I counted, and found that it came to around only five hundred men, with a dozen or so gillies to look after the horse-flesh—most of this being only ponies. And this was the army that was going to free Scotland? I could see no hope at all of this ever happening—until, that is, on the day that the black friar came riding into camp.

It was early in the morning of that day. But even so, the king, the Black Douglas, and the lord Edward were already in chain mail and ready for whatever action had been planned. It was clear, too, that they all three of them knew this man dressed in the white robe of a Dominican but covered head to toe in the black cloak that had given his Order the name of "the black friars."

"Brother Anselm!" the Bruce exclaimed, while the Douglas sprang immediately to help him off his pony.

He was old, I saw then, and also very wearied—not surprisingly, since he had just covered all the long distance from the coastal town of Ayr. He had ridden hard, too, because of the urgency in the news he had brought—bad news of the man who had not only defeated the Bruce at Methven but had since become commander-in-chief of all the English forces in Scotland.

"Pembroke, Sire, the Earl of Pembroke." In a voice as dry and whispery as dead leaves he gasped out the name. "He has received from King Edward of England a written order that says that he *must* take the head of Robert the Bruce. Through bribery, moreover, he has discovered that this is where your army is hidden. And so now he is sending against you a force of fifteen hundred men who will be here, at the latest, by this very afternoon."

I waited, breathless, to hear how the king would receive such news, and after what seemed a long silence, he looked towards his brother and asked:

"Well, Edward? What do you say to this?"

"That we should make a stand!" Unhesitatingly, the lord Edward replied. "Here, where the camp does at least give us a level field of battle."

"No!" Sharply the king contradicted. "That would be to fight on *their* terms, when our sole hope of victory now will always be to fight on the terms that *we* choose."

"What then, Sire?" asked the Douglas. "Should we disperse

31

into a new hiding place—the Forest of Trool, say? And pounce out from there in small groups that will harry and kill as many of them as we can?"

The king shook his head. "Not that either. I have had enough of running and hiding."

He rose, then, and stood staring across Loch Trool to where the great hulk of Buchan Hill towered up from the edge of its steep northern bank. For long he stared, and when he turned again to the others, it was with a look of such inspiration that it seemed not only to light his eyes but his whole face as well.

"We *shall* make a stand," he told them, "but not in the way they will expect us to do so. And it is that hill over there— Buchan Hill—that will be our weapon. What is more, we will win this battle! And so come with me now, brother, come with me, Douglas, and hear me tell the men how we will do that. And Martin—" On the point of departure, he swung round to me. "Stamp out the fire. Clear the tent. Make the whole place look deserted."

Off he strode, closely followed by the other two. I rushed to obey his orders, and it was not until I had done so that I thought beyond these. I had the king's surcoat and spare linen draped over one arm. Slung by a leather strap around my neck was the one thing that *had* to be saved—the small wooden chest holding the circle of gold used to crown him King of Scots. But what should be my next move? What if the friar had been wrong about this attacking force?

"Brother Anselm . . ." Uncertainly I turned to the friar.

"You are sure, are you, of what you told the king?"

"Why do you ask?" He had remounted his pony by this time, and there was challenge in his downward gaze at me. "If the king depends always on the truth in the news I bring him, why should you not do so?"

I looked away from him and towards where the king was addressing the men now gathered round him. Giving them orders for the coming battle, I supposed, but his voice too distant for me to catch the sense of these. The friar, meanwhile, had turned his pony's head towards the army. I stared at this, and could not help blurting out:

"You are off to the battle too? But why? You are no more a soldier than I am."

"Quite," he agreed. "I am a religious. But it is the outcome of that battle that will decide the king's next orders for me. And meanwhile, there may be much else for me to do there. You understand me?"

I did, of course, and it was that very fact that sent the cold sweat of fear trickling down my back. There would be deaths today among our men, many deaths. That, with our army outnumbered three to one, was bound to happen, and it would bring comfort to some, at least, to have the friar there to shrive them of their sins before they died. But what of myself?

Should I go with the army and risk being a victim of that slaughter, or should I try to hide from this great horde of English soldiery? But what if they found and captured me? That meant they would capture also the crown of Scotland, the crown the king had trusted to *my* keeping. And oh, the shame there would be in that! I looked up at the friar setting out so calmly to the possible fate I so much dreaded for myself, and begged him:

"Brother Anselm, what shall I do now? I—I am afraid to die. And yet—"

Mutely I held out the little wooden box at the end of its leather thong, and knew immediately from the look on his face that he was both aware of its contents and had understood the thinking behind my question. Yet still the set expression of his wrinkled face did not soften, and there was harshness in the whispery old man's voice that told me:

"If you had seen what I have seen of the slaughter and famine of this war, if you had seen even one tenth of the misery that Edward of England has brought on our people, you would be afraid of nothing—of *nothing* except of failing in your duty to God, and to our king."

Duty. There it was again, the very word that had brought me into the king's service, the word that once again left me no choice! And finally accepting then that this was so, I followed the friar as he flicked his pony on towards the horses and gillies bringing up the rear of the army's forward march.

I saw Sean then in one of its ranks, and waved to him. He waved back, grinning and holding aloft the spear he was carrying. He's spoiling more than ever for a fight, I told myself sourly, and looked forwards to where the king was leading the march towards the east end of Loch Trool.

Our marching columns swung left to cross over the flat

and boggy ground of the loch's eastern shore. Ahead of us then was the two-hundred-foot-high northern bank of the loch, and a scrambling climb up this steep, uneven slope brought us at last to the foot of Buchan Hill.

An ugly-looking thing it was, too, shaped like an inverted pudding bowl, and all of it made of loose black stone that showed not even a trace of greenery. Its thousand-foot-high bulk loomed up so close to the edge of the bank that there was no room for us to reassemble at its foot. But that, apparently, was not what was intended.

With the king still leading the way, there was yet another scrambling climb, our feet all the time slipping on the broken stone of the hill's surface. The horses, I noticed, were being led meanwhile around the shoulder of the hill—presumably to some gulley where they could stand concealed—and the black friar was riding with them. I looked up from my glance at this to see the Bruce reaching the flattened ridge that made the hill's summit, and heard him shout from there:

"I have brought you to the field of battle. Now let me see you fight!"

But *how* would they fight? I saw Sean among those around me and worked my way towards him to put my question.

"How?" Sean repeated. And broadly grinning then, he began telling me the king's plan of battle.

He was teasing, I thought at first, just as he had always teased me. But there, for once, I was wrong. It was just that he was amused by the simplicity yet sheer audacity of the plan, and the more he spoke of it, the more I felt my spirits rising. It *could* work, I realized. It *would* work—provided our men had the daring to carry it through. And certainly there was no lack of that among them!

I hurried to join in the work of preparing for it, heaving and tugging at boulders to be gathered into piles on the hill's summit. Big boulders, the Bruce had instructed, and that work was hard. My hands rapidly became blistered. My shoulders ached from the repeated effort of lifting heavy weights. Nor was I alone in this.

More and more I heard others cursing the same problems. Besides which, there was no water to be had there. And so, when the order to stop piling up the boulders was given at last, we were all being tormented also by thirst. But we still had no time to think of that, because it was only minutes later that we saw the opening signs of the battle to come.

First came a signal from the low ground at the east end of the loch—a flag waved by some outpost the Bruce must have left on watch there. A lookout man on the hill's summit responded in kind. The order came for everyone to lie down in concealment between the mounds of boulders. I found myself alongside the Douglas, and heard him mutter, "Now the fires! The fires!"

Sean had not mentioned fires. "Sir?" Puzzled, I looked at the Douglas. He pointed downwards, and moments later I saw wisps of smoke beginning to rise here and there away to the east of the hill's foot. The smoke grew thicker, rose higher, and briefly he explained:

"Decoy fires, lit by some of the gillies."

So here was the last and most essential link in that auda-
cious plan! The English would see and follow the broad
trail of our march from the deserted camp. From the loch's
northern bank they would see the smoke of what they were
bound to assume were the fires of our new camp. And then,
all unaware of our hidden force just waiting for them to do so,
they would be enticed into trying to continue their march
along that narrow strip of ground at the foot of Buchan Hill.

I switched my gaze from the smoke to fix it instead on the
loch's low-lying eastern shore. And at last I saw them, a long
column of English soldiers marching four abreast, spears at
the slope, helmets glinting in the afternoon sun. They were
keeping good order, and moving briskly. I felt the roughness of
a boulder beneath my hand and, without meaning to do so,
gripped all the harder to it.

The enemy army reached the foot of the loch's northern
bank. They broke ranks, just as we had been forced to do, to
climb this. I heard their voices, calling to one another, cursing
the steepness of the climb. And joking, too, over the lesson
they were about to teach this miserable little band of rebels.

The first few hundred of them reached the bank's summit
and began trying to reassemble there. But there was not
enough room, of course, to allow that. And always there were
more and more men reaching the top of the bank. The narrow
space between the bank's edge and the foot of the hill became
a confusion of milling bodies, with officers pushing and shouting as they tried to bring their force back into order, but it was
not until this mass of men was as close packed as it could

be that the Bruce rose suddenly to the full extent of his great height, and roared:

"Now throw! THROW!"

As one man our five hundred sprang to their feet, each of them, as he rose, heaving a boulder downwards. It was an avalanche of rock, some of the boulders hurtling straight down onto the heads below, some bouncing off the side of the hill and collecting other stones as they bounced. And again, and again, and again without pause, as if the hillside itself was exploding, the boulders were sent hurtling down with the same smashing force.

The ground at the foot of the hill became littered with bodies heaped every way against one another. Men newly arriving at the top of the bank were struck and thrown backwards over its edge. Nor was it until I became suddenly aware of the noise from all this that I became aware also of the boulder in my own hands. Not to mention the fact that this was only the latest in all those I had already thrown!

I dropped the boulder. It was like a chorus from hell, that noise—the shouts from the men all around me, the screams, the howling, the demented yells of those below lying in a contortion of shattered limbs and bleeding heads. I put my hands to my ears to try to shut out the sound of that hellish din, but still could not muffle my conscience for my own part in the suffering below. Another sound penetrated—the voice of the Bruce suddenly roaring:

"On them, now! ON THEM!"

The response was a concerted yell so loud that it drowned

every other sound. Instantly on this I heard the ring of steel from swords withdrawn from scabbards, saw the flashes of steel from scores of spears leveled for action. Then, and again like an avalanche breaking, but an avalanche this time of men, the charge began.

They were yelling again as they charged, stones scattering from under their feet, yet still with all of them reckless of falling headlong on the hill's loose surface and every throat open on its repeated war cry of *"Bruce! Bruce! THE BRUCE!"* I saw the lithe figure of the Black Douglas in the forefront of the charge, and leaping level with him was that of the lord Edward. But ahead even of these two was the Bruce, his height, his glinting chain mail, his great sword held aloft, all making his downward plunge look like the attack of some huge, avenging angel. As, indeed, to those below he must have seemed.

They put up only token resistance to the ferocity of that charge. Yet how could it have been otherwise for men already unnerved by those boulders? With no room, either, to re-form themselves into fighting order, the battle was not only short but almost unbelievably bloody. They broke and fled from it, leaving us with total victory—just as the king had planned should happen when he thought of using Buchan Hill as the weapon that would turn their own superior numbers against them.

I watched them as they scattered. But rather than the pursuit and slaughter I expected also to see, there was instead a call to the Bruce army to regroup for the march back to camp—a call that was promptly obeyed. Nor did I find the reason for this till I had joined in that march.

"Because pursuit would have scattered us." Briefly, the man beside me answered my questions then. "And what chance would a man alone have against any group of them that turned on him?"

That made sense—a great deal of sense, considering how much the king needed every single man of his little force. I spoke this thought aloud. The soldier nodded agreement to it, and added to his nod, "Aye, it's a good leader that knows just when to mix caution with boldness. And our Bruce"—a tilt of his spear indicated the king now once again at the head of the army—"he knows that better than any leader we've ever had."

I looked along the marching columns, no longer wondering that men still in the fever of fighting had shown such prompt response to the recall. All of them, I realized, every single man in that little army, had learned to have total trust in its commander. The events of that day had taught me what a brilliant commander he was. And it was with that knowledge sending a surge of elation through me that I began at last to share in their hope that "our Bruce" might yet succeed in his otherwise hopeless attempt at making us once again a free nation.

Chapter Four

Sean, *I found*, had been wounded. Not seriously, no more than a gash in his left arm, yet still he was proud of his wound. I bandaged it for him and he strutted off wearing the bandage like a badge of honor.

I fought for the Bruce, said that strutting walk. *See how well l I fought!* I smiled at this before hurrying on towards my duty of attending on the king—only to find him engaged in the kind of argument I had not at all expected.

"But why *should* we leave Glen Trool," the lord Edward was demanding of him, "when we have just won a victory here—and a decisive one at that!"

"That victory," the king contradicted, "was *not* decisive! It was no more than a successful ambush. And much as my old enemy, Pembroke, will be dismayed by that, it still leaves us in no better position than we were before."

"But no worse, either," retorted the lord Edward. "Our army, after all, is intact—thanks to that recall order you gave—and so can defend itself just as well against any other force he may send."

"But not in the same way." Quietly, as always, the Douglas spoke his thoughts. "Because we certainly cannot expect the tactics of Buchan Hill to work *twice* against the English."

"Quite so," the king agreed. "Nor is skulking here in this mountain country the way to the kind of victory I *must* have now—the kind that will persuade more men to rally to me."

"Which is something that cannot be achieved," said the Douglas, "until we have challenged Pembroke to do his worst against us. And for that"—with cold determination now in that quiet voice, he finished—"we *must* leave Glen Trool."

"Exactly!" His tone even more vehement now, the king again agreed. "You have spoken, Douglas, the very words in my own mind."

"But not in mine," objected the lord Edward. "Our position here means that Pembroke has not been able to deploy cavalry against us. But once we are out from among these mountains, he most certainly will do so. And how can we combat cavalry?"

"By planning for that!" The king's face was now suddenly alight, lively with ideas. "By laying a bait for him to attack us, a bait that pride will not allow him to refuse. But that attack, when it comes, will once again be on ground of *our* choosing. And I think I know exactly where that ground will be!"

Quickly he swung around to me. "Martin, tomorrow I am sending Brother Anselm back to his friary in Ayr. Go fetch him to me. And Martin"—his voice calling after me stopped me in my tracks—"tell the friar also that you will be going with him."

I made off to obey the order. And so it was that, with one battle only just ended, I found myself about to take part in the king's planning for the next one.

I had been instructed on what I must do in Ayr. So also had Brother Anselm, and it was with secret pleasure in the thought of what at least part of this would mean for me that I rode on my way with the friar.

That pleasure died, however, when we turned our ponies' heads northwest on the road to Ayr and I began to realize that the rich farmland around us then was strangely empty of cattle and sheep. I saw, too, that all the houses were no more than burnt-out shells, and when I wondered aloud over the cause of all this, the friar grimly told me:

"The cause, boy, was the Earl of Pembroke. Because this is the road his men took to attack us in Glen Trool. And Pembroke's orders from the English king are that, against any who might even be suspected of supporting the Bruce, he must burn, slay, and raise the dragon."

"Raise the dragon?"

The friar shook his head over my ignorance. "When an army goes into action," he explained, "each man there fights under the banner of his own knight, and each knight under the banner of his own lord. And so that is how the size of an army is judged—by the number of banners it brings to the field. But when there is no flag flown except one that has a dragon on it, that means one thing only—total war, with no prisoners taken and no mercy shown to any living creature. And that is what has happened here."

I looked around again at the terrible evidence of what those English soldiers had done on the way to their defeat at Buchan Hill, and was suddenly no longer ashamed of having heaved boulders at them. I thought of the Bruce's army now marching almost due north to his chosen ground for the next battle. I sniffed the wind, a salt west wind blowing in from the coast, where the Earl of Pembroke ruled proudly from the castle in Ayr. And grimly through my mind ran the words:

But pride will yet have a fall. And I am glad, this time, to help in bringing about that fall!

I felt a great deal more cheerful again after that. And all throughout the rest of the long ride to the Dominican friary in Ayr, I was once more looking forward to my time in that town.

Ayr, I knew, held a meal market, and a cattle market, also a fish market that was supplied by the boats in its very busy little harbor. And so, from the very beginning of my time there, I joined each day in the gossip going on among the groups of idlers always to be found in such places. My contribution to the gossip of each group, also, was always the same.

I was a country lad, I volunteered, come to town to see if I could earn a few pennies—come from a farm near Loudon Hill. And did they know about the Bruce army now being encamped at Loudon Hill? Had they heard that the Bruce had challenged the castle governor to battle there? Or that he had sworn Pembroke had only to come out against him to get an even worse hammering than he had given the English at Buchan Hill?

The friar, meanwhile, was retailing the same gossip in the castle, so making it even more certain that the challenge it carried was bound eventually to reach Pembroke's ears. But evenings, for both of us, were different. Evenings were for the pleasure I had promised myself. With darkness in the streets and the Town Watch on the alert to arrest all idlers, those were the times when the friar carried out the king's order to give me some further schooling.

I pored over the manuscripts he brought me, discovering new words, new connections between one word and another, all the time delightedly thinking, *This is life—my life, the kind I want to lead!* Yet still, for all my enjoyment then, I kept on the alert for my ultimate task in Ayr.

I was up from my desk on the instant, accordingly, on the evening that saw an agitated Brother Anselm coming straight from the castle to gasp out, "Pembroke—the Earl of Pembroke, Martin. He has taken the bait laid for him. At last he has taken it!"

In the same gasping haste he went on to tell of the enormous new intake of troops to the castle, and of the gossip there that this was the force to be sent against the Bruce at Loudon Hill—a vastly greater force than the one defeated at Buchan Hill. But even more important than this hugely increased number, much more important, was the warning that Pembroke's attacking force would include a five-hundred-strong body of cavalry.

"Cavalry!" the friar repeated, hurrying along at my side towards the friary's stables. "Just as the lord Edward feared would happen! And when did foot soldiers ever win against cavalry?"

I mounted the pony I had been keeping saddled in readiness. He gripped its bridle to call up to me his last warning: "And tell the king also that it looks as if he now has no more than a few days to prepare for the attack."

All my instincts then were to ride as quickly as possible. But Loudon Hill was around forty miles away, and I could not afford to risk killing the pony by pushing it harder than a fast trot. That meant it was near the beginning of a new day before I reached the sentry who took me eventually to the king, and the king himself had to be wakened to hear my news. I gave this as quickly as I could, all the while anticipating the dismay it would cause.

But there, it seemed, I had been wrong. Rather than looking dismayed, the Bruce simply nodded with a sort of grim satisfaction, before thanking me and advising that I should now have some sleep. Yet how *could* I sleep till I knew just why my news had not seemed to disturb him?

I went off to hand my pony over to the gillies, and just as I had expected, they were more than willing to enlighten me. I listened in wonder as they told of all that had been done to prepare for the battle ahead. And just as had been the case at Buchan Hill, I was once more left with nothing but admiration for the ingenuity of the strategy the Bruce had planned for Loudon Hill.

I did manage a few hours' sleep then, and went out afterwards to survey for myself the terrain on which the battle would be fought. Sean found me there beside the lookout men on the crest of the hill, the gillies having told him of my return. But he knew even more than they did of the planned strategy, and immediately began to describe it for me.

"There!" One pointing hand drew my gaze to the lower part of the long green slope leading to the road running past the foot of the hill. "That is where we, the spearmen, the main body of our army, will take up formation. The swordsmen and axemen will be on either side of us, all ready to follow our lead in the charge. And there"—flinging his arm leftwards, he pointed to the bluff of dark-brown rock overlooking the eastern side of the slope—"there, where they will get the best shot possible at the English cavalry, is where our archers will stand."

I nodded understanding, but still could not help asking, "But what of the odds against us being the winners in all this?"

"Odds, little brother?" Sean mocked. "What do odds matter if we fight as well as we did at Buchan Hill? Besides which, I would have you know, the fame of our victory there has brought another hundred of men into our ranks."

So now it was six hundred against—how many? I speculated aloud on the actual figures before I asked, "And yet still you are not afraid?"

"No." Firmly, Sean gave his answer. "Not so long as there is the Bruce to lead us."

He meant that too, I realized. He had been in teasing mood when he answered my question about odds, but now he was serious. Now he was more like the scarred veteran I had marched beside after the battle of Buchan Hill—the man who had led me to understand the implicit trust the whole Bruce army had in its commander. Sean, in fact, was no longer just the cocky one of the family always spoiling for any kind of a fight. Instead, like the rest of those who were with the Bruce in his struggle, Sean now understood just why and for what he was fighting!

We had another two days of waiting after that, two tense days when the whole army drilled hard and the preparations were constantly being checked.

"Because this time," I heard the Bruce tell the men, "I am staking everything on the challenge I have issued. And Pembroke, damn his eyes, is my mortal enemy. Which means that nothing—nothing at all—can be left to chance."

I was detailed to lookout duty, along with some of the gillies. A piece of rag tied to a stick served each of us for a signal flag. Our orders were to form a chain of signalers all the way up the hill, and at first sight of the English army to relay down this chain the signal of its approach.

I climbed to my position on the summit of the hill wondering why, at the end of those orders to us, the king had said, *"And may God be with you all."* Had that been no more than

48

a formal blessing on our task? Or could it be that in spite of all his planning, he still had secret fears on the outcome of this battle?

It was cold on that summit. I had to crouch down against the wind always whistling round me. My eyes watered with constant straining towards the road along which the English army would come. I ate the last of the bread I had brought with me and grew very hungry. I dozed fitfully when night fell, and was glad when the gillie next in line to my position came occasionally to join me. He was Ewen, a redhead a little younger than myself, and squatting down close beside me on his first visit, he said quietly, "I'm afraid, Martin. Are you?"

I was. But should I make Ewen perhaps even more afraid by confessing that to him?

"I'm tired, and cold, and hungry," I told him. "But you know what the king has planned. And we can trust to that, surely, to see us safely through."

Ewen gave a sigh of what I took to be relief before he went off again into the eerie half-light of the hill's crest. I had reassured him, it seemed. But who, for the rest of this uneasy watch, would reassure me? I peered down into the darkness that held the Bruce in the camp below me and wondered if he, too, was having such a restless night.

I had heard him before, muttering in his sleep the name of the little daughter locked up in the Tower of London. I had witnessed, in my own home, the depth of his feeling for her. Was he sleeping tonight that same haunted sleep—one made even more uneasy by thoughts of the huge army he had now to face?

That army, on the third day of my watch, came at last. I saw the cloud of dust that gave the first sign of its approach. I sprang to my feet, furiously waving my flag. The redhead, Ewen, immediately took up the signal. From gillie to gillie strung out in line on the slope below us, the signal was re-layed. And with all the great speed that practice had taught them, the Bruce men took up their battle stations.

I heard a rumble of sound—the kind that could only have been made by some huge force on the march. And then the English cavalry came into view. I gasped at the sight. And racing up to join me as I stood staring there, Ewen shouted:

"Those horses, Martin! What d'you think of beasts like *that*?"

I had no answer for him. All I could do was just to stand there staring, beginning at last to believe everything I had heard about the kind of warhorse ridden by the English.

The *destrier*, it was called—or so I had been told—and each one weighed a ton. Each one, also, was a stallion—something that, in itself, made it a formidable weapon of war. And now, with a mailed and helmeted knight astride each of them, here were five hundred of these monsters!

As for the road behind this fearsome spectacle, so thick was this with foot soldiers, so far did these marching columns stretch, that the road itself was lost entirely to sight. Yet among all that entire mass of foot soldiers and cavalry, I could see only one banner flying. It was a big one, white and square, and sprawled across the white was a design in red. The banner flapped in a wind that turned it to spread stiffly out with its red design facing towards me. And even distant as it was from me then, I could identify the shape of that design.

A dragon! They had raised the dragon! I gripped Ewen's shoulder, and out of me came pouring all my rage at the devastation I had seen on the road to Ayr, all the fear of what that dragon banner meant for us now. Nor was there any need to explain my outburst to Ewen, because he had also spotted that banner. And Ewen, it seemed, knew as well as I did the meaning of it for ourselves as well as for our army.

In trembling silence, we watched the cavalry arriving level with the foot of the hill. They halted there to deploy into a four-deep rank stretching the whole breadth of the hill's face, all with lances held erect in a veritable forest of shining points. The English foot soldiers, meanwhile, had begun forming up on the ground behind these ranks.

The Bruce army, throughout all these maneuvers, had remained unmoved from its battle order—three separate formations, just as Sean had described to me, standing near the foot of the hill's slope. A horn call sounded from the midst of the English cavalry. I still had one hand on Ewen's shoulder, and felt him flinch from the sound, just as I did. The five hundred knights lowered their lances to hold these couched underarm, and urged their mounts forward.

The horses, as their weight demanded, moved slowly at first. Then, as they gathered pace, and gathered pace again, the charge became like some gigantic wave of steel and horseflesh surging irresistibly forward, the couched lances thrusting glittering points ahead of the wave, the divots of grass churned by huge hooves flying out behind it.

It would take only minutes, I knew, for that charge to reach the foot of the hill. Yet still the Bruce army stood, unmoving, in its formations. I glanced swiftly from this towards the archers stationed on the bluff to the left of these formations.

They were shortbow men, all of them—only the English, so far, having been introduced to the use of the vastly more powerful longbow. But even a shortbow can shoot strongly enough to pierce chain mail—providing, of course, that the arrow is fired at its proper range. And the Bruce, I knew, had given explicit orders on that!

"Oh, hold your fire," I muttered. "O God, make them hold their fire!"

My prayer was answered. The speeding wave of cavalry came into the archers' range—all of them standing with bows drawn, ready for that exact moment. In a whistling, stinging flight of barbs, their arrows rained down on it. But it was not only arrows that accounted for the sudden breaking of that wave. More than that—much, much more than that—was the fact that the cavalry had reached the point where the Bruce had timed the archers' attack to coincide with an infinitely greater hazard.

With yells from the riders, and screams from the horses, the foremost among these great heavy animals came crashing to the ground. They struggled there, unable to rise again, trapped in the carefully concealed pits the Bruce army had spent the past two weeks digging in the boggy softness of the terrain between the road and the foot of the hill.

It was working, the Bruce plan was working! With both of us shaking now with excitement rather than with fear, Ewen and I watched while the riders in the second and third ranks of the charge tried hard to pull their mounts back from the disaster of those hidden pits. But, of course, there is no man on earth can halt a ton of horseflesh barging on at full gallop!

In quick succession, those second and third ranks of the cavalry also went crashing into the pits. And with the archers still raining down their arrows, the magnificent power of that charge was reduced to a ghastly disorder of horseless riders and riderless horses all helplessly thrashing about in peaty mud.

All of them, that is, except for those who had formed, as it were, the core of that charge—those whose place had been at the center of each rank. They had firm ground beneath them—the one strip of ground the Bruce had deliberately left undug. Those in the final rank of the cavalry, also, had managed to wheel aside just in time to avoid disaster.

"See them!" Ewen yelled, one arm outflung towards this remnant. And I did see them, falling in now behind the cavalry's central core still continuing its charge on the narrow front that was all that the Bruce had left to it.

"But see him too!" I yelled in return, pointing down towards the Bruce. And so at last came the moment for which he had so carefully planned and patiently waited.

He was placed, as always, at the forefront of his army. But

this time, his sword was still in its scabbard. What he held, instead, was a weapon long enough to outreach the thrust of a cavalryman's lance—a foot soldier's spear. He raised the spear. His voice—that stentorian voice—roared out a command. Then, with spear held level before him, he bounded forward.

With all the sudden speed of a flood released by some violent breaching of a dam, his army followed—first the spearmen directly behind him, then the axemen and the swordsmen. The archers, too, came scrambling down from the bluff to join this flood. And fearsome as his army's attack at Buchan Hill had been, that still could not compare in ferocity with this latest one!

I saw what happened to the first of the cavalrymen to die—the fourteen-foot length of the Bruce's spear stabbing so violently forwards and up towards this rider that he was sent crashing from the saddle. But it was impossible, after that, for me to distinguish individual actions—impossible to make out more than the fact that the narrow causeway to the hill had become a turmoil of horses rearing, of weapons flashing, of more and more mail-clad bodies being sent hurtling through the air.

It was a relief, all the same, not to be able to make out all the bloody detail of that confused scene. Because that, I knew, would have been just too much for me to stomach. I was glad, too, that it did not last long—mere minutes, in fact, before the causeway was littered with the bodies of cavalrymen and with dead or dying horses.

When did foot soldiers ever win against cavalry? With Brother Anselm's worried question repeating in my mind, I muttered aloud, "Here! Here at Loudon Hill," and looked towards where those who had managed to stay mounted and alive were riding as hard as they could to where their infantry had been drawn up.

Yes, *had* been drawn up, because all of that force, too, was now breaking up—shocked by the cavalry's defeat, panicked into flight by the sight of our army now racing towards *them*. Already, in fact, the Bruce, had victory firmly in his grasp. And just the kind of victory, too, that he had said he needed! I nodded towards the fleeing infantrymen and told Ewen, "It's over for us—see. And so I'm off now, back to camp."

"No!" He seized my arm and pointed down to the *destriers* left stamping aimlessly beside their dead masters. "Not while there's plunder like that to be gathered. And so come on, Martin!"

Dropping my arm, he ran, whooping, down the hill towards the other gillies now converging on the *destriers*. And suddenly feeling in myself the same joyous urge expressed in his whooping, I too ran to help in snatching these first spoils of battle.

Chapter Five

I had not long to enjoy the high spirits that victory had bred in all of us. Ten days afterwards, a mere ten days, the king told me, "I have decided, Martin, to send you with Brother Anselm on another mission. This time, into England."

England! But England was not just the country that bordered on my own. It was the bogey land of all my childhood nightmares—the land that had sent the soldiers who killed my father!

I gaped from him to the friar, quite speechless at first with dismay, and then could not help blurting out:

"To spy for you? Because he *is* your spy, is he not?"

"In everything concerning the English." Calmly the king agreed. "But now he is old and frail, while you, Martin, are young and strong. Also, you are no fool. And so, should some evil chance befall him, he must have such as you to bring back word of whatever he may have discovered."

"For which purpose," the friar added, "you will assume a

role you have already played at the abbey where you learned your letters. Or so, at least, you have told me. You will be the altar boy who assists me when I have occasion to say the service of Mass. Also, since it is not fitting for an altar boy to carry arms of any kind, you will travel without even your bow and hunting knife."

"But Sire——" In even greater dismay at all this, I turned to protest to the king. "The purpose of this mission. You have not yet told me that. And surely I *should* know what it is."

He rose and stood looking down at me. "Martin." His voice heavy with reproof, he spoke his last words on the subject. "What you do not know, you cannot be forced to tell."

He was warning me in the very way my mother had warned the rest of the family on the day I had saved him from the hunters with the bloodhound! I thought of the sore beating I had suffered that day, and was thankful then to be left in ignorance. But even so it was the very fact of the danger implied in his warning that made me all the more watchful as the friar and I began our southward journey to that bogey land of England.

Our route was down the valley of the River Nith—good sheep and cattle country. And yet, I noted, there were strangely few of these here.

"But that," explained Brother Anselm, "is because this route through Nithsdale is the quickest and easiest one for English troops marching north to their various garrisons in our country. And plundering as they go is, of course, the common practice with such troops."

And so that, I thought, accounted also for the sullen and dejected look of the people in all the villages we had passed through. Yet still, it was not until we had stopped to seek our first night's lodging in an isolated farmhouse that the full meaning of it all was borne in on me.

The woman who opened the door to us said doubtfully, "I can give you shelter, but"—she glanced at the five small children peering shyly at us from around her skirts, and finished—"alas, sirs, I cannot feed you."

"No matter," the friar reassured her. "We have bread in our saddlebags." He turned to me. "Martin, hobble the ponies and let them graze."

I did as he said before coming into the house with our gear and taking out the bread. I handed a piece of this to the friar and was about to bite into another when I became aware that the children were gathering around to watch us eat. The friar exchanged glances with me. We had just enough bread to last for the two nights he had reckoned we would be on the road, but these children were skinny creatures with eyes that looked huge in their thin little faces. I nodded in reply to the question in the friar's eyes, and took out the rest of our bread.

It was coarse stuff, no more than oatmeal flour mixed with salt and water and baked into the round cakes we call "bannocks." I had just enough to provide one for each of us—if, that is, the friar and I went hungry. But if he was willing to do so, I decided, then so was I.

The children ate greedily—so much so, indeed, that they

would have choked on their first mouthfuls if the friar had not coaxed them into taking each one with a sip of water. And it was while he was doing so that the woman told the reason for their hunger.

All their livestock, she said, had been taken by the English soldiery. And with no stock left to sell at market, her husband had been arrested for failure to pay the heavy taxes imposed by the commander of the Nithsdale garrison.

"And his punishment for that?" Her voice rose on the words to a sort of half-demented shriek. "His punishment, sirs, was to be whipped while they dragged him along at the tail of a cart—whipped till he died! And me left to watch these fatherless bairns starve to death."

She was weeping into her hands by this time, weeping so bitterly that all throughout our next day's riding I could only hope we would not meet again with such misery. I was so hungry, too, that I was more than relieved to find the two of us being sheltered that night by a family that had learned through experience of being looted by English troops.

The cellar below their house, they told us, held barrels of meat from cattle and sheep hastily slaughtered at the first sign of approaching English troops. Both the man of the house and his son, we learned also, were skilled hunters. And when they had no money for taxes, they had always been able to placate the garrison commander with the present of a deer carcass.

Sourly, after he had told us of this last, the man added, "And so have we learned to live under English rule. Like slaves—always with our heads down and our eyes on the ground!"

"But that not need always be so." Quickly the friar responded before he glanced at me and invited, "Tell them, Martin. You have a way with words, have you not? Tell them about Buchan Hill and Loudon Hill. Tell them about the Bruce."

The son of the house, a big, strong fellow of around twenty years, turned curiously to me. "The Bruce," he repeated. "And those names the friar mentioned. We've heard that he won battles there. But how? And how do *you* know about them?"

"I was there. On both occasions. I saw everything that happened then."

I had not expected the thrill of pride that shot through me with that answer. Yet even so, it was still the very feeling that spurred me on in describing these battles as vividly as I could. Nor did I see anything but approval in the friar's face when even this way of telling made it seem that I had just happened to witness them in course of my service to him.

"I said so to you, did I not?" Almost accusingly at the end of my story, the son turned to his father. "I told you it would be worthwhile fighting back against them instead of living here the way you said. Like slaves!"

Swiftly, through his father's grunt of assent, he turned to Brother Anselm and demanded, "Where is the Bruce now? Where can I join him?"

"Go north to the Dominican friary in Ayr," the friar told him. "Say to the Prior there, *'Brother Anselm sent me,'* and he will give you all the direction you need to find the Bruce."

Into my mind flashed a memory of the Bruce telling my mother, *"The longer I fight, the more our people will rally to me."* And before the friar and I slept that night, I could not resist saying to him:

"That young man—the one who intends to join the Bruce. How many more do you think must feel as he did before he made up his mind to that?"

"Enough for the king's purpose." Through yawns, Brother Anselm grunted his answer. "And when the time is ripe, they too will rally to his standard."

I lay for a few moments thinking of the woman whose husband had been whipped to death and wondering if that time would come soon enough to save her and her children from starvation. Probably not, I realized. As for her poor dead husband . . .

"Brother Anselm—" Restlessly, I turned on my straw to face the friar. "That English king—why has he made such cruel laws against us?"

"He comes of a family with a cruel streak in it—the Plantagenets. And of them all, he is the most cruel. Besides which, he claims that Scotland belongs to him—that it is no more than a province of his own country. And he is convinced that stamping us into the ground will make us accept that claim."

Edward, King of England—"Longshanks," as we called him, the "Hammer of the Scots," as he liked to call himself. I lay awake for a long time thinking of this, and fervently hoping that it would never be my ill luck to meet him in person.

It was around noon on our third day of travel that we crossed the border and were at last in England. We rode over moorland, turning west just north of a walled city that the friar told me was called Carlisle, and an hour or so's ride beyond that we saw the low-lying smoke haze from the fires of what was obviously an army encampment.

And such an army it was! The closer we rode to it, the more we realized how huge was the mass of tents and men and horses beneath that pall of smoke. So far did this mass stretch, in fact, that I drew rein to sit gaping in wonder at it. The friar halted beside me.

"And so now," he said, "you *can* be told the purpose of this mission. I brought news to our king that Edward of England had mustered yet another great army of invasion. And here, as you see, that news is shown to be true. What we have to do now, therefore, is to assess the strength of this army, to discover as much as we can of its commander's plans, and—"

"Brother Anselm!" I could not help interrupting then, because I had noticed—as he had not—the three mounted sentries now heading in our direction. "Look out, Brother Anselm!"

His glance followed the direction I pointed, and quietly then, without any apparent concern, he told me:

"Stay steady, Martin. Just stay steady and trust me to see us past these men."

The sentries were now shouting as they rode. Their leader—a heavy-built fellow, bearded, and scowling—drew his horse to a shuddering halt alongside Brother Anselm. He signaled the other two to pull up behind him, and abruptly repeated their shouted demands for a password.

"Password?" In a voice as gentle as the other's had been rough, the friar queried the demand. And then, with a shake of his head, he continued, "I pray you, sir, have you not been taught that we black friars are vowed to bring the Holy Word to all kinds and condition of people? Or that this includes both you and your fellow soldiers? And have you not also been taught that this vow is therefore its own permission to pass wherever God's will directs us to go?"

The leader's gaze flickered over him, watchfully taking in every aspect of the frail old figure sitting hunched in the white robe and long black cloak of the Dominican habit.

"But if you insist"—mild as ever, Brother Anselm continued—"here is my pass." Solemnly, with right hand upraised to make the sign of the cross, he intoned the blessing, *"Pax vobiscum."*

The lead sentry shifted uneasily in his saddle, then glanced to the two behind him. They also, I saw, were now looking uneasy. The lead man turned back to the friar, opened his mouth to speak, thought better of this, and with a shrug of his shoulders instead gave growling permission for him to pass on. I made to take advantage of this permission, but was stopped from doing so by the leader's seizing hold of my pony's reins.

"Not you!" he snarled. "You are no holy man. And so

63

let me hear *you* give the password!"

I sat staring, openmouthed, at the threat so plain on the big, bearded face. What could I say? How could I answer such a demand? The hand holding the reins was transferred swiftly to my tunic in a grip that compressed my throat and pulled my face close to his own. I felt the roughness of the fellow's beard, smelled the sour smell of his breath.

"You heard what I said!" The snarling voice had become even more insistent. "The password! Let me hear it!" Chokingly, I tried to say something—anything—that would buy me a few seconds to think, and heard the sound of my spluttering suddenly overridden by the friar shouting:

"Shame on you, sir, to lay hands so rudely on the lad!"

The grip on my tunic was slackened—enough, at least, to let me turn my head and see the friar. He was seated bolt upright now, on his pony. And suddenly, too, he was no longer the small and frail old man I knew. He seemed to tower, in fact, such was the authority now in his bearing. And so fiercely, too, did his eyes blaze as he added:

"The very lad on whom I will depend to serve at the altar when I am saying Mass for your fellow soldiers—and who is therefore as much under the protection of Holy Church as I am!"

The grip on my tunic was dropped altogether. I saw that the sentries' leader was now staring at Brother Anselm in a sort of fearful amazement. Because now, in a voice of thunderous menace, the voice of a preacher in full flood, the friar was continuing:

64

"I gave you my blessing when we met, and would then have continued as peaceably as is my wont. But now, sir, you are trying to arrest my assistant in works of holiness. And it is not for nothing that we Dominicans are known also as 'the Hounds of the Lord.' Hear my pronouncement, therefore, on so sinful an act. Take care, take very great care that it does not cause me to revoke the blessing of Holy Church and to lay on you, instead, her curse!"

The leader shrank back from me. The men behind him threw furtive glances of superstitious awe at Brother Anselm. With a sharp word of command to me, the friar urged his pony on towards the army encampment. I followed him, feeling quite weak with relief at my escape, and glancing back towards me, he pointed at the army ahead.

"Do you see that?" he asked. "The great square tent with the standard flying above it—that can be none other than the tent of the English king, Edward himself. But to find out what may be going on there, we must first establish ourselves among the wives and other women who always follow so large an army."

They were where he had expected to find them, these camp followers—beyond the horse lines and row upon row of heavy supply wagons. And the moment they realized they had a friar among them, they came swarming around us. Some were carrying babies, others dragging young children by the hand. But all of them were babbling a welcome, and it was the very nature of that welcome that gave us the first hint of the information we needed.

The army, they complained, had not only taken a long time to muster, it had been camped there for weeks past, with what seemed little prospect of moving on. And so would not the holy friar baptize the babies who had been born in the course of all this? And would he not also say prayers for those who had died since leaving home?

"But why *has* there been all this delay?" asked Brother Anselm. "Your army is here to invade Scotland, is it not? And so why does it not proceed with that?"

The women exchanged glances that made it seem they were almost frightened to speak, but one of them did volunteer at last:

"Because the king is sick—very sick."

Brother Anselm was off his pony by that time, and so was I. He handed me the leather bag that held all he needed for saying Mass, all the while making sounds of sympathy to the women before he told them, "But first, in all this, from any of you whose souls are not clean enough to partake of the Mass, I must hear confession."

The women started obediently to kneel, one by one, before him. I unpacked the leather bag that held the wine and bread for the Mass, the chalice for the wine, the paten on which to place the bread. I donned the white surplice he had also brought for me in my role as altar boy. But everything that followed the friar's command, the confessions, the Mass itself, the baptisms, the prayers for the dead, took a long time—too long!

I slept like the dead myself on the straw of the lean-to the women provided for shelter, my stomach comfortably full of the food they had also provided. I woke only slowly, also, when Brother Anselm shook me next morning and hissed in my ear:

"I am off to discover what I can by talking to the men and their officers. Now get up! You have no friar's habit to protect you in spying on this camp, and so must find your own excuse for doing so."

My own excuse? I looked around as the friar set off towards the rows of army tents, and noticed the bundles of firewood stacked beside the supply wagons. With one of these on my back, I reckoned, it would be taken for granted that I was just another of the many camp orderlies they must have. Bent under that load, too, my face would not be observed. And yet . . .

To venture alone into the very midst of the enemy! I breathed deeply to try to calm myself, hoisted the firewood onto my back, and set off towards the English soldiery.

They were different from our men. That was the first thing to strike me. Ours were lithe and sinewy, their actions swift, their faces gaunt with hard living. These men were solid of flesh, with round and ruddy cheeks, and all their movements had a sort of deliberate slowness. Their accents, also, sounded strange in my ears. But it was too risky, in any case, to linger long enough at any campfire to overhear what might be said there. I would have to depend on my eyes alone to inform me, I decided, and with head down but glances still darting everywhere, I continued through the camp.

It stretched before me, a seemingly endless muddle of tents and men and campfires. Yet still, at the end of a whole day of trudging from one part of it to another, I felt I had gathered a good knowledge of this army's weapons, its numbers, and the disposition of its forces. Out of all I had managed to note, too, the one thing that most dismayed me was its company of archers.

That company, I reckoned, amounted to some two thousand men. All of that two thousand were armed with the weapon the English had learned to use from their wars against the Welsh—the longbow. And longbows had such range and power that two thousand of them could wipe out our little army in a matter of only minutes!

I turned away from the archers thinking of the hope that had risen in me after Buchan Hill, the joy of victory against all the odds at Loudon Hill, and the pride I had suddenly felt at having been part of all this. It was that flash of pride, I realized, that had told me how committed I had become to the Bruce cause. But now that cause really *was* doomed.

My back was sore with the weight I had carried for so long. In my heart was a different kind of pain. I trudged back to the supply wagons wearily accepting that there was nothing more I could do—except, possibly to spy on the cavalry. And yet, I wondered, what was the point of that when even I could see that, once those archers had done their work, this English king would not even need to deploy his cavalry against us?

With a sense of duty driving me, all the same, I dropped

my load beside the wagons and joined in the task of watering the horses from the river winding past the camp. There was a whole horde of men and boys going up and down with their buckets, after all, and so no one was likely to challenge me at this.

I counted the cavalry as I went. I made it the same number as that of the archers; and utterly wearied as well as despondent by then, I went back to our lean-to shelter. The women had left food there for us. I set half of this aside for the friar and ate hungrily of the rest. But the friar, when he returned to the lean-to shortly afterwards, did not even touch his share of the food. Instead, speaking very rapidly and grimly, he told me, "King Edward is more than very sick. He is dying!"

"What did you say!" In pleased surprise, I shot upright to stare at him.

"You heard me. The talk among his officers is that he may not even last the night. And so it is that we must seize what could be our last chance to hear him speak of the plans he has for this army."

"We?"

"Yes, 'we.' You will be there with me to add cover to what I intend. But also, if my true purpose in this is detected, so that you can try to stay free for long enough to escape back to the Bruce with word of all we may have heard."

I felt the food I had bolted down beginning to rise in my throat. I swallowed hard and got rid of the impulse to be sick. I donned the surplice he handed to me. I took up the bag that contained the sacraments of the Mass and followed him from our shelter.

I did all this, too, with feelings that were strangely mixed. There was elation in the thought that the English king was dying. But there was also fear in the knowledge that, in only a few minutes, my greatest dread would become a reality. I would meet face to face with old Longshanks, the Hammer of the Scots. And what if that fear proved the stronger of these two feelings? How would I acquit myself then?

Chapter Six

It was still light when Brother Anselm and I left our lean-to, but the rain that threatened had made the sky dark and lowering. I kept my position behind him as he wove a way between the camp-fires, and as befitted my role of altar boy, I walked with eyes modestly downcast. He halted at the king's tent. I looked up then. My gaze traveled up the tent's huge bulk stretching away towards the flag flying its red and gold against that lowering sky, and I felt a moment's dizziness.

Low in his throat, the friar said, "Courage, Martin!" and raised a hand in blessing to the two sentries on guard at the open flap of the tent. The sentries waved us on. I took a deep breath to steady myself and followed the friar into the tent.

It was like stepping into some half-lit cave filled with foul air. I gulped against the stench—a most appalling one of vomit and decaying flesh mingled with that of some foul herb and the stink of grease from the candles—and looked towards the great bed at the center of the tent.

71

There were groups of men gathered at a little distance from each side of it. All of these were most splendidly dressed, with jewelry sparkling against the smoothness of their satins and velvets. They, I guessed, must be the courtiers of the English king, and their faces as they stood murmuring to one another were full of deep and anxious foreboding.

There was one man, however, who stood alone and who towered above all the others there—towered by reason of his headdress, which was that of a bishop's miter. It shone with gold, this miter, it glittered with jewels. The man who wore it stood clasping the rail at the foot of the bed. His dress was also of gold, a golden cope richly embroidered with thread of green and scarlet.

Brother Anselm pushed a way towards this splendid figure, myself closely following. Kneeling then, the friar seized one of the hands clasping the bed rail and kissed the huge purple jewel of the ring on this hand. The figure looked down on him as he said rapidly:

"My lord bishop, I beg you leave to say Mass for the healing of this great and most afflicted of kings."

The face under the miter was plump and fat lipped. Its eyes were small and mean. The mean glance shifted from Brother Anselm to me. On a note of faint surprise, the fat lips uttered, "A wandering friar! And with an altar boy all ready for the Holy Office, no less!" Quickly I also knelt. And with the surprise in his voice changing to sarcasm, the splendid one questioned Brother Anselm:

"And what good, little brother, do you think *your* prayers

will do when mine have failed to heal the king?"

"None, I should think, unless God so wills." Meekly, ignoring the sarcasm, the friar responded. "But as I have found before, my lord, it is not always through the mighty that He works this will, but often also through the poor and humble."

The fat lips took on the shape of something that could have been a smile but that looked to me more like a sneer. "This king," they mouthed quietly, "insists he has business yet to finish before I give him the last rites. And so pray away, little brother. Pray that these may not be needed yet awhile."

The mitered head turned from Brother Anselm to look once again at the figure in the bed. My kneeling position, with my nose close to the struts of the latticework at the foot of the bed, enabled me also to look at this figure. And so it was that, at last, I saw him—the bogeyman of my childhood, Edward Plantagenet, most cruel of all his cruel family!

Yet how wasted he was now with illness—those legs, those long legs of his so lean now that they hardly raised the coverlet of the bed! His face, too, was the color of dirty clay, with cheeks all fallen in to leave chin and nose sharply jutting. His hair, straggling down on either side of that sunken face, was white. And, indeed, it was only his eyes that seemed to give the lie to all this.

Those eyes, sunk deep in his head as they were now, were still sparking fire. And that fire was directed straight at the young man who stood beside his pillow, holding one of the sick man's hands in his own.

He was tall, this young man, and long legged. His hair

73

was golden, his physique nothing short of magnificent. He was, in fact, the image of what—or so I had been told—the English king had been in his youth. Also, he was so much more richly dressed, even, than all the others there, that I knew he could be none other than this king's heir—his son, Prince Edward. Yet still, for all his high standing, he was flinching now at the words that came along with that fiery gaze.

"Promise me," the sick man was insisting. "If I do not live to invade Scotland again, you will lead the army in my stead."

The demand had been voiced in what was not much more than a rasping whisper, but that was still enough to silence all murmuring from the groups of courtiers. Enough, too, to still the sound of prayer from Brother Anselm. Yet even so, I realized, this magnificent-looking young prince was hesitating to give the assurance it sought.

Once again the whisper was painfully rasped out from the sick man's throat, and this time it was answered. The prince nodded and then, in a low voice, he said:

"Your wish, Sire, is my command. I do indeed promise."

King Edward sighed. His eyes closed, and for a long moment his whole face was still. Then, gradually, the muscles of it began to work. Bubbles of spit appeared at the corners of his mouth. The spit trickled down his chin, and from his lips came a long, low mumble of sound—a stream of words that finally became stronger and clearer, until not only I but everyone else there could tell exactly what they meant.

This king, this old king so visibly rotting to death, was

using the last of his breath to claim once more that Scotland belonged to him and to him alone—that it was no free kingdom, but only a province of England. With that last of his breath, too, he was cursing Robert the Bruce for trying to take Scotland from him. I tried hard to ignore this tirade, and was thankful when another voice broke into it—the voice of the gorgeously dressed cleric at the foot of the bed.

"Sire!" In genuine dismay this bishop was pleading now. "You have little time left in this life, and so I beg of you to use it to better advantage. Make your peace with God, Sire. Make your peace with God."

The eyes of the dying man flew open. With an effort that drew a murmur of protest from the crowding courtiers, he raised himself to direct his gaze not at the bishop, but once again at his son. At the end of this effort, too, he continued that interrupted litany of hatred against the Bruce.

"And what is more, this Bruce must *know* as he dies that it is I, Edward, who have killed him. Because, my son, when I die and you lead my army into Scotland, you will carry my bones at the head of that army!"

Prince Edward gasped aloud—as, indeed, did everyone else there—yet still could not take his eyes off the fierce gaze holding his own. Nor could he disengage his hand from the clutch of the one that still held it. There was a distinct tightening of that grip, in fact, as the king insisted:

"Promise me you will do that, my son. Promise that you will carry my bones at the head of the army."

"I—I—" Falteringly, Prince Edward began his answer.

And then, as if trying to resolve this situation as soon as possible, he said quickly, "Yes, yes, I promise, Sire. I promise."

The old king's mouth opened on a long sigh of satisfaction. He fell heavily back onto his pillow. For several moments he lay like this, his breath now coming out with a loud, rattling sound, his eyes directed in a stare at the canopy above him. The rattling suddenly ceased, but his eyes remained open, and I was still anticipating what he might say next when Brother Anselm dug me sharply in the ribs.

"Get out," he whispered. "Our work here is done, and it will attract notice now if we do not join in their mourning."

He rose as he spoke, then began to sidle past the shouting, wailing throng of courtiers pressing in on the bed. I followed, moving in the same furtive way and only then fully realizing what the sudden end to that rattle of breath had meant. Edward, King of England, Hammer of the Scots, at last was dead!

"This new king, Brother Anselm—this Edward the Second of England. Will he keep his promise to the first Edward?"

We were back in our shelter before I dared voice that question, but all I got in answer was a shake of the head.

"Because, if he does," I persisted, and went rapidly on from there to tell him of all I had observed that day. He listened in silence, but nodded from time to time as if to say I was doing no more than confirm some observation of his own; and quite exasperated by this at last, I burst out:

"Will you not tell me then? What will we do if he does keep

that promise? What will happen if he does march?"

The friar lifted his head to give me a long and oddly sad look before, very abruptly, he said:

"I have heard from the Bruce that it was you who saved him on the day he was hunted by his own bloodhound. But how do you think the hunters got hold of that hound? And who were they?"

I shook my head, astonished by his questions, but still no more able to answer them than on the day of the hunt itself, and with seeming pity for my ignorance, he told me:

"Those hunters were MacDowells of Galloway, the southwestern province that borders on the Bruce's own earldom of Carrick, and it was from a raid on Carrick that they got that hound. The MacDowells, also, are strongly allied to the Bruce's most bitter enemy. And you do at least know who *that* is."

I did, of course. Everybody knew of the long hostility between the house of Bruce and the house of Comyn, just as everyone knew that this hostility was rooted in rival claims to the throne of Scotland. I looked at the friar and named the enemy aloud.

"John Comyn, Earl of Buchan."

"Aye." Sourly the friar agreed. "Buchan, most powerful of all the nobles in Scotland's northeast, more powerful indeed than any other in the whole country, but also the one man who will never acknowledge the Bruce to be our king. So now you know who it was who set the MacDowells on to stealing his hound and then using it to hunt him down."

I stared at the friar, visions of that hunt fleeting through my mind. He nodded, as if aware that this was so, and grimly added:

"Let me remind you, too, that both Buchan and the MacDowells have managed to stay in power only by consenting to become tools of the English. And so guess for yourself now just what will happen if this English army does invade. Guess at what the king himself already half knew and wholly dreaded when he sent us on this mission."

It was so easy to guess—the Bruce caught between two forces equally intent on crushing him out of existence, the English coming up from the south, and Buchan taking advantage of that to come down on him from the north. I sat in silence, groping through my thoughts for some way out of this dilemma, and suddenly remembered the young man who had volunteered to fight for the Bruce—the young man from Nithsdale.

"But wait, Brother Anselm. Wait! If the Bruce could rally the rest of the country to him, if he could create a general uprising—"

The friar's hand uplifted for silence cut short my cry.

"It is still too early in the Bruce campaign," he told me, "for that to happen. There will be uprisings here and there, of course, no doubt of that. But the country is so firmly in the grip of the English that most of it, as yet, will be too afraid to come out openly for him. On the other hand—" He paused, his wrinkled face becoming even more wrinkled with thought.

"On the other hand—" Slowly he repeated himself. "If

this army does not invade—" Again he paused, and then, in a spurt of seemingly renewed energy, he went on, "The Bruce, in that case, would be free to march north, free to make the first strike against Buchan and Buchan's allies, and thus to totally subdue them. And so *that*, Martin—"

He grinned at me, his old face lit now by a sort of gleeful malice, "That is what you and I *must* find out now—the answer to your question of whether or not the new English king will keep his promise to the old one."

"But how?" I looked in bewilderment at him. "You cannot, surely, find any excuse for going into the new king's tent?"

The friar began settling himself for sleep. "Of course not," he agreed. "But what do you think will be the talk of the whole camp, among soldiers and camp followers alike, now that old Longshanks is dead?"

There was no more to be had from him that night, I realized. But had he not already as good as told me what my share in our task should be? He, in his friar's habit, could mingle with the army as freely as he chose. But I could not do so at all without being remarked as an interloper. It was here, among the camp followers who had already accepted me as his companion, that *my* work must take place. And already I was clear in my mind on what would be the key to that work.

I lay back in my straw thinking of the plump faces of the soldiers I had seen that day. I thought, too, of the talk I had heard in the Bruce army—the talk from which I had learned that these English were constantly amazed to discover how our men could both march and fight on no more than a handful of oatmeal a day. But that, as I had also learned, was because the Englishmen would not even march, never mind fight, unless they were sure of an ample ration of beef, and ale, and bread, and cheese.

They would get none of those things in Nithsdale! Grimly I reminded myself of that. As for the rest of the country, the English garrisons there had already squeezed as much provision as they could out of it. Besides which, the women had said, this new army had already been long on the road. The very size of it, also, argued that old Longshanks had been set for a major campaign. Yet how, in heaven's name, could a poor country like ours sustain them in that?

"Supplies . . ." That was the key! I settled for sleep, muttering the word to myself, and was up the next morning all ready with my plan of action.

Daily I began to loiter near the supply wagons—but not so near that anyone could challenge my purpose there. Daily I watched as men came up to draw rations for their various companies, and though I was not close enough to overhear much of what was said, I could still recognize the anger in the arguments that took place between these men and their army's quartermaster.

Daily also I began to make myself useful to the women who had fed and sheltered the friar and me, collecting wood for their fires, fetching water for them, or carrying heavy baskets of washing to and from the river. Just as I had thought would be the case, too, they were talking in the same way as

I had guessed for the men at the supply wagons—every one of them complaining bitterly over shortage of rations.

"Well done, Martin," the friar approved when I reported these findings to him. "Very well done."

But that was at the end of a whole week in which he had said nothing to me of what he might have discovered, and with something of resentment at this, I asked:

"And you, Brother Anselm? What have you found? This new king—what have you learned about him?"

"The new king?" Brother Anselm gave a shrug of obvious contempt. "This Edward the Second," he said, "is held by high and low alike to be not at all the man his father was. Think what else you like about him, old Longshanks was still a great soldier. But from all that I have heard, his son is interested only in fine clothes—and in such as share his taste in these!"

"But will he march?" I persisted. "Will he keep his promise in spite of his army being so short of supplies?"

Brother Anselm shook his head. "The old king spent fourteen years of his life trying to bring Scotland completely under his thumb, and so *he* would certainly have risked doing so. But this new king cares nothing for soldiering, and even less for soldiering in Scotland. I do not think he will march. Not this time, at least."

I saw him only once again, this new king, before his army finally struck their tents and turned south. He rode at the head of it, a tall figure, bright and splendid in his silks and satins as a peacock with tail outspread. Behind him rode a group of nobles only a little less splendid than he was. But hoisted shoulder high on a platform behind them was a bier that carried a lead-lined coffin. And in that coffin was the decaying body of King Edward the First of England.

The signal to move off was given. The supply wagons rolled. The long columns of men began on their march south. The friar and I sat on our ponies, watching all this happen. I listened to the creak of the wagons, the thud of the marching feet, and thought, *There it goes, all that great army, with the taste of retreat now in every man's mouth. And there he goes, proud Edward no longer, but just instead a heap of rotten flesh and bone.*

Brother Anselm spoke aloud, quietly, his words at first coming like an echo of my own thought. "There they go at last. And there"—with the quiet voice rising to a sudden note of triumph, he pointed towards the peacock figure riding first in the cavalcade—"there at their head is the weak fool who has just given our king the very chance he needs to turn now on the enemy at home!"

We had seen all that we needed to see. We turned our ponies' heads, and with the friar's words as valedictory on our mission, we began the ride back to Scotland.

PART II

The Lion As Hunter

Chapter Seven

S ean and I, before our army marched north against the Earl of Buchan, were given home leave.

"In renewal of my thanks to your mother," the Bruce informed us, "and also to let her see how you have prospered under my command."

As indeed we had. Before he turned to deal with the Buchan forces, the Bruce had secured his back by raiding so fiercely in Galloway that he had more than revenged himself on the MacDowells for the way they had hunted him with his own hound. The success of these raids had also yielded us much of the weapons, money, and clothing that his army had once so sorely lacked.

So there were Sean and I now, each of us carrying over one shoulder the long and warm woollen plaid we would need against the cold of a Highland winter. Sean, in addition, now had the kind of padded jerkin that gave the ordinary foot soldier at least some kind of protection against enemy weapons.

He had also acquired a helmet and a sword. And proudly, as we rode along together on the ponies we had borrowed from the horse lines, he kept one hand on the hilt of this sword.

He talked all the way home of those raids into Galloway, of the battles in which he had fought, of the castles the Bruce army had stormed and then set on fire or otherwise destroyed. Moving always with such speed, he was at pains to add, and striking with such surprise, that the MacDowells had never known when or where to expect the next attack.

I listened to him with little or nothing to say in return, my part in such matters having been simply to act once again as the Bruce's page.

True, I had managed to secure a proper tent for him out of the spoils; also a fur cloak and some much-needed linen. I had served him in other ways, too—notably by keeping a tally of all the stores we had won both in coin and in kind. It was true also that all this had greatly pleased the Bruce. Yet none of it had given me any of the kind of heroic stories that Sean continued to tell until the very moment we were breasting the hill that led to home and he felt, as I did, the smoke drifting rankly into our nostrils then.

I sighted the source of the smoke before he did, and just as I had feared, it was not coming from the chimney of our house. It was from the house itself—or what was left of it!

We spurred our way up the hill, all the time hoping that one of the family would come running to meet us to say that they, at least, had escaped the fire. We saw no one. We heard nothing. All we saw was the house with its timbers caved in, and the smoke that rose from the thatch lying askew on the fallen timbers. All we heard was the sound of our own frantic breathing. As we slid from our saddles in front of the ruin of the house, Sean spoke shakily the hope to which I, too, had been clinging:

"Maybe they all managed to get out before the fire happened."

We stood for a moment exchanging looks that silently asked, *But did the fire just "happen"? Or was it deliberately set?*

"We must look," I said. He nodded agreement, and together we stepped through the smoke haze hanging over what had been the doorway of our home.

We saw them almost immediately—the bodies of our mother and Morag lying sprawled amid blackened rubble. Both were naked. Both were grotesquely streaked with the dark red of blood that had dried over massive wounds. Sean turned his head aside and retched, the sound coming up from the very pit of his stomach. I stood in silence, transfixed with shock. And then, with thought slowly returning, came also my realization of the meaning in what we saw.

Raise the dragon! That was the order that had gone out against all who were thought to be supporters of the Bruce. And this was the result of it for *our* family!

"Martin!" Sean was grabbing my elbow with one hand, wiping vomit from his lips with the other. "Shona! What about her? Where is she?" Wildly he glanced around—as I did too, his words jerking me into horrified expectation of what there might yet be to find among the ruins.

We searched then, but without finding Shona there.

"But maybe she escaped before they came." Sean looked at me with something like hope beginning to replace the wild expression on his face. "And maybe she found somewhere to hide but is still too afraid to come out."

He made for the door and began stumbling towards the outbuildings, calling out Shona's name. I followed him, joining in with his calling. We separated after we had searched the outbuildings, and for the next hour each of us went his own way poking and prying into every possible hiding place that Shona could have found.

Farther and farther afield my own search went, out to the tangle of scrub west of the house, north to the stream where our goats always drank and where she had watched them there, from a little cave she had found in its bank. Distantly, as I searched, I heard Sean calling Shona's name as constantly as I did. But when we met again at the house at last, he had no more to report than I had.

"But we cannot go back to camp until we do find her," he insisted.

"No," I agreed. "We cannot. But neither can we leave here, Sean, until we have disposed decently of our dead."

Sean stood for a long moment, his face working, his eyes suddenly blind with tears. And then, with a great, shuddering sigh of acceptance, he turned from me. By common consent then, as it seemed, we both took from our shoulders those warm woollen plaids that were to have been our protection from the Highland winter.

We shook the plaids out to their full length. Sean laid his over the body of Morag. I laid mine over my mother's body. But there was no way that we could dig a grave for either of them. The raiders, as we had already discovered in our search for Shona, had not only cut the throats of our sheep dogs and driven off our cow, our sheep, our goats, our geese. They had also destroyed everything that could be of possible use to us.

There were no spades, nothing at all that could be used for digging, and so there was nothing for it but to carry the bodies outside, where we could build a cairn of stones over each one. We took Morag first, then went back for our mother. But when it came to piling over our mother the stones we had gathered, I told Sean:

"Wait, Sean, till we have placed her lying facedown." He looked up at me, startled, not realizing why I had said that until I added, "Remember, Sean? She was a poet."

He understood then. He began to sob, great dry sobs that shook the whole of his body all the time he was helping me to lift her and lay her on her face. Together, we began covering both bodies with stones. Sean's sobs, by the time we had built a cairn over each of them, had turned to silent tears. But as for me, it was as if the flood of tears I wanted to let loose had been frozen by the horror of it all.

I stood back when we had finished and looked at the cairns. No fox or wolf would gnaw now at either Morag or my mother. No further harm in this world could be done to this strong and gentle girl who had always been such a good elder sister to me. No further harm could come either to my mother—the mother who had so unselfishly sent us both off to fight for freedom, and who had paid for that, now, with her own life.

I looked again at the cairn that covered her. I had dreamt once of my mother lying facedown in some cold and dark place—lying dead. But this, here, was no dream. This was my nightmare come true! Sean's voice broke into the horror of that thought, Sean pleading with me, "Say the words, Martin. *Requiescat in pace.* . . . Come on, you have book learning. You know how it should go on."

I knew. I had read often enough, at the abbey, the prayers for the dead. I had listened too, to Brother Anselm saying the requiem. I repeated them all quietly, the prayers, the psalms. Sean joined in where he could. And then we went again to look for Shona.

It was the very uppermost slope of the hill that we searched next because, we reasoned, it was really only from there that she could have spied the attackers in time to hide from them. Remembering, too, that this was the time of the year when she was accustomed to gather rowanberries, we narrowed our search to the most likely places for these. And it was in one such place that we did eventually find her.

A basket half full of berries, with other berries scattered around it, was our first clue. The next was one of her shoes marked with the stains of dried blood. We followed a trail of tall grass spotted with the same kind of stains. And there she was, lying almost but not quite hidden by the thin stems of young rowan trees clustered all around her.

She made no movement at our approach. Her eyes were closed. Sean dropped to his knees to bend over her. Her eyes flew open, their gaze fixing on the helmet he wore. She screamed, and screamed again. Sean gripped her shoulders, shouting, as he tried to calm her. She screamed all the more, and tried vainly to writhe out of his grip. I seized him by the collar of his jacket and jerked him away from her, yelling as I did so:

"Your helmet! That's why she screamed. It makes you look like one of them—the soldiers who did the killing. And that's what she takes you for." I pointed to Shona, now desperately trying to scramble away from us. "Look at her! See how out of her mind with terror she is even yet!"

Sean stared from her to me, in bewilderment at first. And then, with understanding following on this, he removed his helmet. "Keep very still now," I told him, then went on my knees in front of Shona. She was crouching as far away from us as she could, her gaze shifting from Sean to me and then back to Sean again. And gradually too, I saw, the terror in that gaze was fading—but only to be replaced by something that was no less heartbreaking.

As her terror died, indeed, so also did the life of her mind seem to die, until her gaze had changed to one that came out of nothing and was directed also towards nothing. I spoke then, trying to coax something out of this emptiness.

"It's Martin, Shona. Your brother Martin. I've come to help you gather the rowanberries."

Shona's nothing gaze took on something that might have

been a gleam of understanding. Slowly it shifted in the direction of the place where we had found the basket of berries. Her gaze lingered there, then came back to me. And in her usual clear, sweet voice, but now with the puzzled look of one trying to remember something, she said:

"The ones I already gathered, Martin. I dropped them somewhere."

"I'll help you find them." I glanced from her to Sean, only then fully realizing how truly I had spoken about her. She *was* quite literally out of her mind with terror. But she had at least now recognized me, and that had surely accomplished something! "Sean will help you, too," I added, and boldly challenged him, "Will you not, Sean?"

"If she will let me!" It was to Sean's eternal credit then, I am sure, that he said this in a good imitation of the cheerful bluster so usual with him. He even managed a laugh before he added, "Because both you and Shona know very well how cack-handed I am over small things like rowanberries!"

"Oh, Sean!" Shona protested. "I never said so."

Sean threw a swift glance at me. *At last!* said the glance. *She has recognized me, too, at last!*

He bent with me then to help her rise. She cried out at this, a cry of pain. And it was then that we saw why even her terror at first sight of Sean had kept her crouched there instead of trying to run from us.

The foot that had lost its shoe was awkwardly twisted in a way that warned of a damaged ankle, and in the calf of the other leg was the deep gash that had left the trail of blood we had followed.

"We'll carry you," I told her. "Sean and I will carry you down the hill, Shona."

"No, no!" Frantically she pushed away my reaching hands. "Not down the hill! Not down the hill! The soldiers— they're all there. The men with the swords, the torches! They'll kill me! They're waiting to kill me like they killed Mother and Morag—the men, the men, they're still there. . . ."

On and on she went, moaning and screaming the protests that bit by bit unfolded the full truth of her experience. She *had* seen the approach of the raiders, and had hidden from them. But then, after she had also seen them depart driving our stock ahead of them, she had gone down the hill to rejoin our mother and sister—only to find them as we had found them. And now, we gathered from her ravings, she was certain that these raiders were waiting to do the same to her.

We gave up, in the end, on all our attempts to calm her, and when she was finally quiet again, it was only with the quiet of exhaustion. We knelt by her limp form and saw that her eyes had once more taken on the nothing look of one whose mind has gone. And so what was to be done now?

We *had* to carry her off that hill, however much she might scream. But what then? Who would take her in, see to her wounds, give her food and shelter? There was no one we knew who would dare to risk that—not after what had happened to our family!

93

"Bloody English!" Sean burst out, and jumped up, his clenched fists raised high. "God damn them, God damn them all to hell!"

"Sean—" I rose to catch hold of his arms and swung him round to face me. "I know where we can take her. Not down the hill, but up and over the other side to the one place where she *can* be safe. And where she *will* be looked after."

He stared at me, stupidly at first, and then with light breaking into his face. "The nunnery. Of course, the Cistercian nunnery! Martin . . ." He paused to draw himself up, once more the soldier and very much in command of the situation. "Go down the hill and fetch the ponies—"

"No!" Sharply I interrupted. "You fetch them!"

He glared at me. "What was that, you—you little whipper-snapper!"

"You fetch them. That was what I said. And I'll stay here with Shona in case she looks up and goes mad again at the sight of that helmet of yours."

"Hmm." The glare fading off his face, Sean admitted, "You could be right, I suppose. In which case . . ." With a shrug of acceptance, he turned to go downhill.

I sat beside Shona till he came back with the ponies. She was silent till then, but as soon as we tried to mount her, she screamed and struggled against us. Sean solved the problem by swinging her over his pony's saddle, where she lay, quite limp, with all the fight suddenly gone out of her. Sean mounted behind her, and it was like this that we delivered her to the gatekeeper at the Cistercian nunnery.

I looked back as we finally prepared to leave there. Shona had a nun supporting her on either side by that time, but she was not looking at either of them. She was watching us turning to ride away from her, and it was then that I made a vow to myself.

I had been afraid so often since taking service with the Bruce—afraid for myself and what might happen to me in this war. Yet he was still the only man who might be able to defeat these invaders, the only one who could drive them completely from our land. And so come what might, I vowed, I would never again shrink from anything he might ask of me.

Sean did not look back. Sean was cursing again, even before we were out of earshot of the nuns. I did not curse. My blood was as hot and angry as his, but in my mind there was nothing now except a cold determination to keep my vow.

Chapter Eight

Our route towards the province of Buchan lay
along the Great Glen, the huge mountain rift
that runs clear across the country from southwest to northeast. At its northeast end lay
Inverness, the principal town of Moray—the province neigh-
boring on that of Buchan. But Moray was also under English
domination, and so it was only by capturing Inverness and
forcing his way onwards from there that the Bruce could
finally launch his army against Buchan.

But that army now, of course, was a very different one
from the ragged band of freedom fighters in Glen Trool. I
missed many faces from among that five hundred—in
particular that of the Black Douglas, who had been left in
command of a force powerful enough to maintain the hold
already achieved on the southwest of the country. Yet even so,
we were now a thousand strong.

We were, moreover, a well-armed thousand that included
nobles such as Malcolm, Earl of Lennox, as well as Sir Robert

Boyd and others who had once fought beside the Bruce at Methven. Yet terrible as the defeat there had been, they had still dared to rally again to his standard, and the news they had brought with them was just what he had hoped to hear.

The men of Moray—who had long despised their over-lord, the Earl of Ross, for becoming no more than a tool of the English—had now begun open rebellion against him. And the inspiration behind their rebellion? That was their own bishop, David of Moray, the same fiery cleric who, in defiance of all England's might, had dared to crown the Bruce as King of Scots!

"Our first objective, therefore, in all this," the king declared, "must be to aid these rebels by capturing the town of Inverness." And so it was with this for its orders that our army finally started on its march up the Great Glen.

Mountains towered high on either side as we marched. The cold wind of that October howled down from them and over the chain of lochs lying between. Nor did I have any plaid to protect me from this wind or from the rain it brought lash-ing down on us, and so could do no more than set my teeth and endure until at last a halt was called.

It was dark by then, but we had reached a point where the glen opened out to a clearing at the south end of the biggest of all the lochs—Loch Ness. There was some sort of settlement there, but no light showed among the scattering of houses, and hard on the signal to halt, the king called:

"Raise the standard! Shine light on it to let them know who we are."

Torches were hastily lit. Sir William de Irwin, the royal standard-bearer, raised the Bruce standard. The light flared on the scarlet lion rearing at its center, and on our men as they hammered at the doors of the houses. Lights began appearing in the windows there. Doors opened, and gradually through these came the people of the settlement. They stood staring at first, seemingly unable to believe that what they saw really was the Bruce army, and not simply yet another force of the enemy come to raid them. But once they *had* grasped that, they could not have done enough for us.

For the king, they found a barn big enough to house him and his officers, and rapidly had a pile of heather cut to make beds for them. Our men, meanwhile, had begun to light fires, and the women of the settlement moved among these, shyly offering such food as they could spare. They brought food to the barn, too, among it a haunch of roast venison.

The woman who presented this to the king blushed scarlet at his thanks, and seemed to me to speak for the whole settlement when she said:

"We have little enough to offer, Sire, but our blessing to you comes with all that we have."

I ate my share of the food and was about to settle in my usual place at the king's side when he took a sidelong look at my bedraggled state, and said sharply, "Where is your plaid, Martin?"

"At home." Quietly I answered him. "Or at what was my home. My plaid, Sire, is now my mother's shroud."

The single candle the women had left us meant that the

barn was too dark for me to see his face, but I could sense him staring at me. "You have changed, Martin," he said at last. "That look you wear so often now. It makes you seem not just older than when you joined me in March of this year, but"— he hesitated for a moment, then finished—"but somehow also harder."

He was guessing at what I had experienced on that visit home, I realized, and I went on to tell him briefly of what had happened then. I kept my voice low throughout, also, not wanting others to know of so private a grief. And whispering still, I added:

"But none of that, Sire, has made me like Sean—yearning every day for bloody revenge on what was done to our family. And so any change you see in me now can be due only to that vow I took at the end of it all."

"Never again to shrink from anything I might ask of you." Quietly the Bruce repeated the words I had quoted to him, and as quietly added, "That is a good vow, Martin—the best you *could* have made, for your own sake as well as for mine."

We settled for sleep then, both of us, but our rest lasted for only a few hours before dawn saw the army once again on the march. We struck off to the right then so that we could reach Inverness without having to cross over the Ness—the river running out of the loch's northern end. And for the whole of that second day's march we were on high and very open moorland.

The high ground descended to a village lying close enough to Inverness to mean that English troops might have been quartered on the people there, and so we waited for darkness before skirting silently around it. A mile or so beyond the village lay the pinewood where the Bruce had planned we should wait to launch a dawn attack on Inverness. But hardly had we settled into position there when our scouts came racing back to give him a brief and breathless report of their news.

Inverness Castle was already in flames—set on fire by the very man the English had appointed as its governor, Alexander Pilche, the town's sheriff. All the citizens of Inverness, also, were now in revolt against the English, urged on to this by the bishop of Moray, and the town itself had been taken over by an army of no less than two thousand Moray men.

"Martin!" The Bruce turned from the captains who had gathered around him to hear this news and rapped out an order that sent me racing to the horse lines. I heard, as I ran, the horns that sounded the assembly. I saw torches flaring in the darkness. I reached the pony that carried the king's gear and quickly unstrapped the small wooden chest I had saved for him at the battle of Buchan Hill.

All around me, meanwhile, were gillies following shouted orders to loose horses and bring them forward. I loosed a pony for myself and swung into the saddle. There was torchlight falling now on the lion flag of Scotland held high by Sir William de Irwin. I tucked the box safely under my arm and headed straight for the flag.

The assembly, as always with the Bruce army, had been rapid, and each of its captains was mounting now to ride at the head of his own company. As always, too, the king was in the lead of the whole army—but not, this time, riding alone. This time he had with him Sir William de Irwin, still proudly flying the royal standard. I rode forward, boldly, knowing what he had in mind for me, and took my place behind these two. The signal to move off was given, and the army began on its way to Inverness.

With less than a mile to go then, it was mere minutes before we saw flame-reddened clouds in the sky ahead. Then the flames themselves leapt into view. And distantly also, along with this, came the noise from the town—a noise that continued to increase the nearer we drew to the mound on which the castle was perched.

It was huge, this mound—a natural outcrop of stone rising more than a hundred feet high. On all except the side from which we approached, it dropped sheer down to the River Ness or else to the town on the river's east side. The castle at its summit blazed like some monstrous torch in great tongues of red and yellow, and from the dry timber of its walls came sparks that flew out like showers of scarlet stars.

We reached the foot of the sharp incline leading up from our approach. The signal to halt was given. I lifted the key that hung always on a chain around my neck and unlocked the little chest. The Bruce turned to motion me alongside him. I opened the chest. He reached inside it and drew out the circle of gold that was his crown.

In one swift movement, then, he had clapped this over the pointed dome of his helmet and was riding forward up the slope, followed only by Sir William with his standard—and by me. That crown was in my keeping, and there was no way I was going to lose sight of it!

There were bodies lying ahead of us all the way up that slope—the dead bodies of English soldiers. The Bruce rode on without even a glance towards them, heading straight for the burning castle and the two men standing in front of it.

One of these was the Bishop of Moray. Or so I gathered from the way the Bruce immediately dismounted to kiss the ring on the hand extended to him. Yet never before had I seen a bishop dressed for war, and so still I gaped to witness the chain mail beneath the episcopal cope falling back from that extended hand!

The other man was also in chain mail, but openly so, and had his sword unsheathed. He, I guessed, was Sheriff Pilche, the rebellious governor of the castle. He knelt to offer his sword to the Bruce. Gravely the Bruce kissed the sword before returning it to its owner. And then, with a signal to his standard-bearer to go with him, he strode to a point of the mound that enabled him to look down on the town below. I slid hastily from the saddle to gain a similar vantage point, and once again was left gaping at what I saw. At what I heard, too!

From the foot of the mound ran streets that were crammed with figures. Some of these were the town's citizens. Others were soldiers—but not from our army. These were men of Moray, some in chain mail, but even more in the Highland kilt that left bare their brawny arms and legs. Torches flared among them. Weapons were being raised—

swords and axes waving in great circles of triumph—and the tumult of noise from all this was that of uncountable shouts of celebration.

I looked towards the Bruce standing there with the flag of Scotland waving above his tall form, the gold of his crown glittering against the dark metal of his helmet, and realized how clearly visible he was now to all that turbulent mass. He drew his sword and raised it high above his head, the flames from the castle running red along its blade.

Face after face in the crowd below turned up towards the sight of that crowned figure with its fiery blade. And all those shouts, then, ran together into a single loud-roaring version of the same cry I had first heard in Glen Trool—a roar of *"Bruce! Bruce! THE BRUCE!"*

"Martin," the king told me, "I need a courier."

A courier? I stopped, wondering if this was a word from the French language spoken by the nobility.

"A swift rider," he explained. "One who carries messages—in this case, messages of great importance."

The king's swift rider . . . I liked this name, liked the ringing sound of it. "If you trust me to act as such, Sire," I told him, "I am willing."

"But it could be dangerous for you." He paused, looking very straight at me—remembering, perhaps, what I had said to him in the darkness of that barn? I gave him look for look before repeating that I was willing, and with a nod of acknowledgment then, he told me:

"In that case, go choose yourself a pony—after which you will report to the Bishop of Moray."

I chose my pony, a surefooted little mare I had long had my eye on. She was gray in color—not the safest choice for riding at night, but—in the words the gillies used of her—*She runs so fast, she can lose one wind and catch another.* And that, for me, was the deciding factor. I named her "Storm" and rode off on her to report to the bishop.

He looked up at me from the map spread out on the table in his tent—a little man, round cheeked and sharp nosed, but with eyes that glared as intently as those of a hawk.

"You are the king's swift rider? Then hear this. It is not the king's intent to overrun the whole of Moray, but simply to force the Earl of Ross to beg for the truce that will allow the Bruce to proceed to his main objective in Buchan. After which, we have agreed, he will return to complete the work here. Now look at this map of Moray."

Quickly he swiveled the map round for my inspection and drew a finger along the sea inlet edging the north coast of the province. "That," told me, "is the Moray Firth, and all Ross's troops are concentrated on the coastal plain beside the firth—here, and here, and here . . ."

The moving finger began stabbing the map at various points along the coastal plain. "And so these are the points on which swift and sudden attacks will be made by various sections of our army lying in wait near each one. At the same time as each attack, also, part of that same section will raid one of the stores where Ross has laid up supplies for his own troops—thus diverting these to our own army at the same time as he is forced to spread his defenses ever more thinly. D'you follow me?"

"Yes, my lord."

He nodded. "Then study that map, because these attacks will be scattered all along that plain. Nor will Ross ever know just when any of them will take place. And that, my lad, is where you will come in with the swift riding needed to warn each of our commanders just when his attack should be launched."

I bent towards the map. Bishop David rose to leave the tent, giving me a sharp tap between the shoulder blades as he did so. "Study it well," he advised, "or you might feel an arrow soon—just there!"

I finished poring over that map with a whole list of names chanting in my head—Ardersier, Cawdor, Nairn, Auldearn, Forres, Elgin—my whole mind like a map itself with paths, cattle tracks, roads, and visions of towns all etched into it. And for the next three weeks, when I was not at the side of the king, I was riding hell for leather with orders from him to one or another of his commanders.

I enjoyed that time—surprisingly, I thought, considering the way it tested the sense of purpose I had so recently found for myself.

Always, just as I had guessed would be the case, I had to ride at night. And there is nothing like darkness to heighten any sense of danger! My sole guide was the heaving gray of the firth's waters to one side of me—but only so long as I was on the coastal track. The smaller tracks I had to follow when I turned inland were a maze that left me nothing to rely on except the map I had striven to fix in my mind. And never once did I ride without some heart-stopping challenge being flung at me.

From somewhere unseen among the rocks and dunes edging the coastal track that challenge would come, or else from some bearded face looming fearsomely out at me from the heather verging an inland path. I had the password—a different one for each section of the army—and it was very quickly indeed that I learned to snap this out in reply to any such challenge. But it was just as quickly too, on the other hand, that I learned how immediate was the response to the orders I carried—and how successful!

Burning castles, kilted Highlanders swinging broad-swords, spearmen charging, archers loosing their arrows—with something like awe I saw how that campaign unfolded in wave after wave of action that grew ever fiercer, ever more relentless. Yet with each town that was taken by our army, I saw also how its people rejoiced to be so suddenly liberated from enemy rule and was glad then of the part I had played in that.

It gave me an odd sense of power, also, always to be riding so fast on Storm. And Storm herself was not only fast and surefooted. She answered so quickly to my touch that often, it seemed to me, she and I were one.

I was proud of her—and in a different way, I was proud too of having so many experienced commanders trusting to the information I could carry so quickly to them. All of them, that, is, except for Sir William Wiseman, the principal commander of the Moray men.

"You are young to have such responsibility—maybe too young." Suspiciously he challenged me when first I brought him his orders, and immediately I threw back at him:

"I am old enough, Sir William, to have earned the king's trust."

That was enough to satisfy him, I suppose, since I did not then have to show him the pass the king had provided to meet just this sort of situation. Nor did I have any further trouble of this kind, my worst fear—as Bishop David had warned would be the case—being that of an enemy arrow in the back.

But Storm, I swear, could *smell* danger. Twice, she stopped short and refused to continue past what I later discovered was concealment for an English sentry post. This, on the first occasion, was a turf wall; the second time, it was a haystack. And so it was not just with pride but with gratitude too that I rode her beside the king's own horse to the meeting that ended that campaign—the truce meeting that the king had finally forced the Earl of Ross to accept.

I watched there while Ross sullenly put his signature to the treaty that Bishop David thrust at him. I watched as the bishop signed as witness to the truce. But still nothing of this concerned me until the king announced harshly:

"And think yourself lucky, Ross, that you have meantime escaped so lightly. Because it was you who captured my daughter. It was you who gave her as prisoner to the English, and—"

"But wait, wait!" Frantically, his face paling suddenly under his beard, Ross tried to interrupt. "I did not know how cruelly your daughter would be treated by her English jailers. I swear I did not—"

"Silence!" Contemptuously, the Bruce cut off this protest. "I will have no more such pleading from you. But what I will have, what I must have, is some better guarantee to this treaty than your signature. And you know, do you not, what that means?"

Ross stood for a moment staring at the implacable expression on the face opposite his own. Then, in a low voice, he gave an order to one of his retinue. The man walked quickly away to disappear among some more of the earl's followers, and then returned leading a boy with him. The boy looked up at the earl with wonder in his face, and also fear. Ross did not return the look. Instead, in a shaking voice, he told the Bruce:

"My son, Walter. He is not quite fourteen years old. And he is all the hostage I can offer."

"But will have a kinder fate with me," rejoined the Bruce, "than ever my daughter had with you." And with a glance back at me, he ordered, "Martin, take charge of this child."

I went to do as I was bid. And speaking low as I led the boy away, I said, "You know what will happen if you try to escape our army?"

He nodded. "My father's life will be forfeit."

I wished then that the look in his eyes was not so much

like that in the eyes of Shona when I left her at the gate of the Cistercian convent. Yet still I managed to push from my mind the feeling this gave me and to think instead of the only thing that mattered now—our coming campaign in Buchan, and the victory we *must* gain there.

Chapter Nine

It was late November before we could start the march from Moray into Buchan—entirely the wrong part of the year for campaigning. Yet still we had to take advantage of the time afforded by the truce.

In the face of a bitter wind and blinding snow we headed over wild hill land to the small market town of Inverurie. There, for a long time past, the Bruce had owned land, and he easily found one of his farmer tenants who was glad to house him and his officers. But there, too, we were overtaken by the worst of all mischances.

The king fell ill—too ill to continue in command. And Inverurie was dangerously close to the border with Buchan!

On the lord Edward's orders, we made a litter for him and marched north again, carrying him with us into the friendly territory of Strathbogie. But Strathbogie lay so high in the hills that the cold there simply increased his illness. We had no medicines for him either, and food for the army ran so short that there was little even for him.

There was nothing for it, it seemed, but to return to Inverurie. But our presence, by then, had been sniffed out by a company of Buchan archers. We took the king into the shelter of woodland where their arrows could not reach him, and for days after that, our archers skirmished with theirs. But this could not last, of course. And in the end, it was only a bold sortie by the lord Edward that set the Buchan men on the run and allowed us once again to reach Inverurie.

I had walked close to the king's litter each time we moved him, the boy Walter keeping faithfully by my side. When the king would otherwise have lain exposed to bitter cold in the so-called shelter of that woodland, I had shielded him with my own body. Yet now, even after we had once again reached the comfort of the house where he and his principal captains had earlier stayed, he still continued so desperately ill that it seemed certain he would die.

And what then would happen?

It was the lord Edward who would have to continue the struggle, and he was the kind of soldier that others would gladly follow. Yet it was not soldiers alone who could win freedom for Scotland. It was also ordinary people like this kindly farmer and his wife, sensible people like my dead elder sister—even poor frightened souls like my little Shona. And poets—poets like my dead mother!

On all of them, as I had already seen for myself, the magic that was somehow in the Bruce would always work as much as it did on the men he led. But there was no magic in

111

Edward. And that, I knew, was the final answer to my question. If the Bruce did die, so also would the hopes and dreams of us all.

I watched and waited beside him, changing his sweat-soaked bed linen, bathing him with cold water to try and bring down his fever. The farmer's wife and servants helped me with this, exclaiming all the while over the mottled flush on his face, the way he had to gasp for breath. The boy Walter—seemingly paying no heed at all to the fact that he was the son of an earl—gladly fetched and carried for us all. And gradually—miraculously, it seemed to me—this terrible illness became less and less.

From sitting up in bed and taking some nourishment, the king began at last to be able to walk again. And to talk! To start planning again, indeed, with the captains who had come in every day to see him, and finally to hold a proper council of war with these.

Bluntly then he reminded them that we were already at the start of the day before Christmas, and that too much time had already been lost. The word from our scouts, also, was that a Buchan army was gathering at the village of Meldrum, only five miles away. And so it was essential, was it not, for us to go once more on the offensive?

"And we will," the lord Edward assured him. "We soon will." To which, more cautiously, Sir Robert Boyd added, "But not, Sire, till you are fit to ride again."

"I will be fit," the king rejoined, "when *I* say I am fit."

It was almost, I thought, as if he had spoken in prophecy,

because it was just then that a scout arrived to report that a patrol from the Buchan army had overrun one of our outposts, and that its commander, Sir David Brechin, was even now preparing an attack in force. The king stared at the scout. And then, with red rage flooding the paleness of his face, he roared out commands for "general assembly" to be sounded and for his horse to be brought.

He was struggling to rise as he did so, but the others there tried to restrain him, anxiously insisting that he was still not fit to ride. And truly, he was not. He swayed as he stood trying to beat their hands from him. The gauntness of his face was once again pale. Yet still his voice rose above theirs, hoarsely declaiming:

"Nonsense, I tell you! Nonsense! This is the best medicine I could have had! And the worst for Brechin—because he thinks me helpless and so will never expect *me* to lead the counterattack!"

They had to yield to him in the end—if only out of fear that this very exertion would make him drop dead where he stood. After which there was nothing any of us could do except to help him dress and arm for the battle ahead. With a hand commandingly held out to me then, he ordered:

"Martin! My crown!"

His crown? Never before had he worn that while riding into battle! That night at Inverness Castle, in fact, was the only time I had ever seen him wearing it. And so what did he intend now?

He sat with the circle of gold in his hand, not looking at it, his gaze impassively fixed on some middle distance. The boy Walter and I watched him, the boy's eyes as wide with question as my own. Sir Robert Boyd and the Earl of Lennox came in to help him to his feet, but he brushed them both aside and rose of his own accord. In the same way, then, as he had done at Inverness, he jammed the crown over the pointed dome of his helmet. And grimly with this gesture, he declared:

"The Earl of Buchan challenges my right to the crown of Scotland. I ride now against him, therefore, as Robert, the true and lawful King of Scots. Let his army see that, and beware!"

He had drawn himself fully erect with the words. But when he then tried to step forward, he staggered. And with looks of dismay flying between them, Boyd and Lennox supported him from the room. I followed them out to the maelstrom of activity now all around the house—armed men mounting, gillies rushing up with other men's mounts, and beyond all this the milling mass of our army forming its battle positions.

The king was in the midst of all this, and it was taking the combined efforts of Boyd and Lennox to hoist him into the saddle. But even when they had succeeded in doing so, they had to edge their own mounts close to his so that each could reach out a hand to steady him.

"Quick, Ewen!" In panic at this sight, I turned to the gillie beside me—the redhead who had kept watch with me on Loudon Hill. "You and I are also going to this battle!"

He gawped at me. "But the customs of war do not allow gillies to fight!"

"We are not going to fight!" Impatiently tugging at his sleeve, I shot the words back at him. "We are going to observe, and maybe—if the worst comes to the worst—to try to save the king's life!"

That was enough for Ewen. Like all the gillies, he would do anything for the king, and together we raced to the horse lines to loose and saddle ponies for ourselves. I had my own Storm. He had the little black creature I had rejected in favor of her because, although it was fast, it was known to be a biter.

"Over there!" Ewen pointed ahead and to our right. "That rise they call Barra Hill. It's halfway between here and Meldrum, and so we'll see everything from there." We began racing neck and neck to where he had pointed, with myself gasping out as we did so, "How do you know all that?"

"How d'you think?" Ewen twisted in the saddle to grin at me. "I was born here—on a farm not far from our camp beside the River Urie!"

Away to our left I saw the dark mass of our army steadily moving at an angle to the course we had taken, cavalry in the lead, the royal standard fluttering high above the cavalry's front rank. In my mind, I ran over the strength of that mass, and wondered if the Buchan force would outnumber it.

Seventy horse—that was all we had of cavalry. As for the rest of the army, we had suffered considerable losses against the Earl of Ross. As planned, also, the Moray men had stayed

115

behind to guard our backs against treachery from that quarter—all except for Sir William Wiseman, who had brought us three hundred of his Highlanders to make up for our losses. Once again, therefore, we were a thousand strong. And these Highlanders, I reminded myself, were famous not only for their charge with the broadsword but also for their fearsome skill with axes—all of which made them a most formidable replacement!

Barra Hill, a green mound of around two hundred feet, loomed up in front of Ewen and myself. He took the lead, guiding the way to a point that gave us a sweeping view of the countryside around. It was all moorland, broken here and there by streams, and with only slight rises and falls to it. Good terrain for a cavalry charge, I thought, and strained to see what I could of the Buchan army.

It began coming over a slight crest of ground to our right at the same time as our army did on our left. The Buchan army was headed by a cavalry force that I reckoned as being some two hundred compared to our seventy. Beyond this I saw a mass of foot soldiers that seemed to be about equal to our own, and briefly, then, I thought of my brother, Sean. He, at least, would be fighting on even terms, I realized, but it was still cavalry that would swing the day.

Anxiously I looked again towards our own army, and saw that the cavalry had advanced far enough to let me pick out a close-bunched group of three in its front rank. So Lennox and Boyd, I guessed, were still having to hold the king upright in his saddle—even now, when there was less than half a mile between them and Buchan's cavalry! I bit my lip, waiting to hear which side would first sound the charge.

It came from ours, in a long and deep blast of the horn. Seconds later, like an echo of that horn, the signal came from the Buchan side. The first forward surge on both sides quickened its pace. The blades of lances held upright cut swathes of light through the dull December air. Then suddenly, so suddenly that I gasped to see it, there was a flash of gold at the front rank of our cavalry, and the Bruce was out ahead of it in a burst of speed that had him charging, on his own, at the enemy.

I had seen him before, of course, at the head of a charge— but never, like this, entirely on his own. And never in this sort of situation! He had been so sick—was still sick. Yet there he was now, riding tall and straight as ever, his lance gripped tight, the gold flashing from his head making him seem even taller—a man who was a king in appearance as well as in name, a king riding with all the power and speed of some primal force unleashed!

I saw the front rank of the Buchan cavalry waver at the magnificence of the challenge thus thrown at them. And what I saw then, too, was the magic of the way the Bruce had always been able to inspire his men. They roared, roared instantly on the sight of his charge. They struck spurs to their mounts. And with the royal standard fluttering above them, the sound of their roar still reverberating, they galloped as madly after the Bruce as he was galloping in the lead.

The charge from the Buchan side, at this, faltered even

further. Outnumbering our cavalry by nearly three to one, theirs still could not help but waver at the awesome effect of that opposing charge. And waver again until they broke and scattered, with those on the fastest mounts doing their best to outpace the others.

"And their small folk!" Ewen grabbed my arm, shouting out the local parlance for foot soldiers. "Look at their small folk, Martin!"

I switched my gaze from the charge that had begun to turn now into pursuit of the enemy, and looked to where the foot soldiers of the Buchan army had been drawn up behind its cavalry. These men too, I saw, were now also beginning to scatter—unnerved, I supposed, by the way this had been routed. Our advance party of Highlanders, on the other hand, had immediately taken that as the signal to come leaping like stags over the moor towards them, so that it looked as if they, too, would be routed.

For some minutes, then, both Ewen and I stood gazing alternately from the sight of our Highlanders bloodily wielding their broadswords and axes to that of our cavalry chasing after the Buchan horsemen. But it was the king who was leading that chase, just as he had led the charge against them. And turning at last to Ewen, I said:

"This pursuit of their cavalry, Ewen. How far off is that likely to take the king?"

Ewen shrugged and pointed. "To Fyvie Castle, maybe— twelve miles from here. That's their nearest refuge now."

A twelve-mile ride after the exertion of that charge! There

118

was nothing, surely, more likely to exhaust the energy he had somehow managed to call up!

"Come on, Ewen!" I kicked heels to Storm's flanks, and shouted back over my shoulder. "I have to find the king. I have to be there if he needs me."

Ewen followed as I rode swiftly off in the direction of Fyvie Castle, but we were only two miles along that track before we found that pursuit of the Buchan horsemen had been transformed into a running battle between them and our own cavalry.

Men dismounted and now fighting on foot, clashes between men still on horseback—time and again we had to detour to avoid these combats. My fears for the king grew with every one we passed, but still there was no sign of him.

"And if that is so," Ewen argued, "he must still be leading the pursuit. Nor will he thank us if we find in the end that he is still fit to do so, and so why try to follow him any farther?"

"I do not care whether I am thanked or not." Swiftly, I snapped my answer to this. "And you do not know how far he can push himself on anything he is determined to do. Nor did you see him before the battle—staggering, almost fainting . . ."

I was on the move, even as I spoke. Ewen followed, grumbling still over what seemed to him a pointless effort. But he did at least follow me. Yet still, it was not until we were almost in the shadow of Fyvie Castle itself that we did at last find the king. But then also, and almost immediately so, I saw that he might be in even worse condition than I had feared.

His horse stood riderless, with blood streaks on the saddle-cloth draping its flanks. The king himself lay stretched on the ground, the lord Edward standing over him, Sir Robert Boyd supporting his head, and others of our principal men crowding around these three. I slid from the saddle and ran to worm my way through the crowding figures so that I could kneel beside him.

There was blood on him as well as on the horse—but only splashed on his armor, and not, thank God, leaking through it. He was conscious, too, and again I thanked God for that. But otherwise, as was more than plain to see, he had no more strength left in him. The visor of his helmet had been thrown back to show a face that was ghastly pale. The fairness of his beard was quite darkened by the sweat pouring into it. Yet still, amazingly, he was struggling to sit up and talk to his brother, Edward.

Sir Robert slid a hand beneath one of his shoulders. I helped him raise the other. And half sitting, half lying then, the words came gasping out of him:

"Go on . . . on with the pursuit! Then . . . then re-assemble . . . reassemble the army. March all the way through Buchan. Burn . . . burn its castles, its crops. Slaughter its livestock. Spare no man. Mercy—no mercy save to those who beg for it, and will swear allegiance . . . allegiance to me. Destroy the Earl of Buchan, Edward—destroy him utterly!"

"I will! I swear I will!" Swiftly kneeling beside the king, Edward made the promise. "But, brother . . ." He paused to let a troubled glance rove over the faces of those around the pair of them and then looked again at the king to finish, "What, meanwhile, of you?"

There was a babble of voices then, all assuring the lord Edward that some of them, at least, would stay to get the king back to Inverurie. But how? I wondered. He was no longer fit to ride—not any more than had been the case when he had first fallen ill. And so we would again have to make a litter for him. Or perhaps—?

I looked towards the farm buildings sprawling to one side of the castle, and, gently dropping my support of the king's shoulders, I ran off to get the hay cart that I knew was bound to be in at least one of these buildings.

Chapter Ten

e got him back to Inverurie, Ewen and I, our ponies hitched to that hay cart, an escort of brawny Highlanders marching watchfully alongside. And it was only then that I had time to think about his order to the lord Edward.

Burn! Destroy! Spare no man! Harsh words! More than harsh—they were brutal. And because he was not ill as he had been before, but simply very weak, I dared at last to query them. He frowned at this, and asked abruptly:

"Have you ever before heard me give such orders?"

I shook my head. "Never, Sire. On the contrary, I have always heard it said among our men that you are not like other leaders—that you are too merciful, for instance, to order the killing of prisoners. And that, they say too, is because you are ruthless only when you have to be."

"And one of those times is now." With a nod, and another frown, he emphasized the words. "Because, boy, I am now at a tide in my affairs. I have won all my battles so far. I will win even more—but only if Buchan does not remain poised to strike like a dagger in my back. And so the only way to turn that tide in my favor is to destroy him so completely that he can never again threaten me."

"But his people, Sire," I protested. "'Spare no man,' you told your brother. And so what will become of Buchan's people?"

"They will fight, and fight hard." Grimly he made this prediction. "They know well that their earl is at blood feud with me, and so they will not see any invasion of their territory as part of my war for freedom. To them, it will simply be a clan struggle between Bruce and Comyn."

The king paused for a moment as if to judge whether or not all this had sunk into my mind. and then in a quieter tone he added:

"But if you remember my words so well, Martin, remember that I also told my brother, 'No mercy *save to those who will swear allegiance to me.*' And that, hard as it may seem to you, is the best hope that the Buchan men have now."

So the king I had for so long held to be a hero was *not*, as I had begun to fear, just another bloodthirsty warlord! I felt relieved, if still somewhat shaken, by what he had told me. But to devastate the whole province of Buchan—how long would that take? I wondered aloud about this, and with the frown once more on his face, he told me:

"My brother will have five castles to capture, and he has no siege artillery. It will take something like three months, I fear, to achieve my purpose there."

Three months! That time, I thought, would hang heavy for both of us, and so was all the happier to see our young hostage now so much the king's friend that the two of them were often absorbed in a game they called "chess." I was glad at first also that the Bruce was often now visited by a young man who had come in the retinue of the Earl of Lennox—a sprig of French nobility by the name of Jean-Marie de Picard. But afterwards, I was not so glad.

It was, after all, in de Picard's own language that they spoke together, which made me feel left out of things. I came to resent de Picard's presence, in fact, myself having always before been so close to the king. And it was this, I suppose, that drove me one night to ask why the Frenchman was there at all instead of out fighting with the rest of our army.

"Because, perhaps, he is like you." The king smiled at the startled look this drew from me, and then went on, "In one way at least, because, though he does not want to fight, he does enjoy adventure. And that reminds me, Martin. He has expressed a wish to be my squire, and I have long had need of such. I have therefore granted his wish. And Martin—"

The king paused there, as if hesitant over what he had to say next. Then, abruptly, he finished, "Our hostage, Martin, has changed his allegiance. He has now declared his complete loyalty to me. And as of tomorrow, it is he who will be my page."

Shock would be too mild a word for what I felt then. I had more or less expected, I suppose, his announcement about de Picard. And the boy, young as he was, could certainly be thought old enough to decide for himself the question of allegiance. But for the king so suddenly to replace me with that boy . . . and after all I had gone through since he had first declared it my duty to join him!

"And I?" My voice choking on the words, I managed to speak at last. "What, Sire, am *I* to do now?"

"You, Martin?" He looked hard at me for a moment, then suddenly he smiled—the kind of smile given by one with a pleasant surprise up his sleeve. "You served me well in Moray," he said. "You served so well, indeed, that now I want you once again to be my swift rider, and also to combine that with something more—something much, much more."

Three days later, I was once again in the Great Glen, but this time, I was riding south. Winter cold had frozen what had once been torrents pouring down the rockfaces on either side of me. But the king had seen to it that I was warmly clad, and so light and free did I feel that, if I had been a bird, I would have flown, singing, over it all. I was on my way to that something more he had promised. I was on my way to Ayr, to see Brother Anselm, who would be my guide in that.

"You have changed, Martin." Those were his first words when we finally met—the same words the king had used to me in the dimness of that barn in the Great Glen. "You have a different look to you now—one that makes me think that you have at last learned what war really means."

So he knew about my family! I looked away from him, not

wanting this thought to be shown on my face, and abruptly then he asked:

"But the king—you have come from him, have you not? And so how is he? What news now of his illness?"

I told him everything I knew about the king, and added details on our recent campaigns I thought he might not have already gathered from his usual sources of news. Yet all the time I was doing so, I kept being surprised by how much he already did seem to know. Nor could I help eventually re-marking on this—upon which he smiled his crooked, old man's smile, and tartly responded:

"So! Is that, perhaps, why you are here with me now— to learn more of how I manage that!"

I said nothing for a moment, just looked at him, and thought of the king telling me, *Brother Anselm's network of informants is vital to me, Martin. And this will be a long war—a scattered one, too, with the English so entrenched in all the various castles they command. Yet this friar has already become too old and unfit to travel as he used to. . . .*

"Well?" Brother Anselm was impatient for answer. But I had grown taller, broader, in my time with our army. And he, during that same time, had shrunk even more into his old man's shell. I felt a giant towering over him while I told what the king now required, and was both relieved and pleased when, through a cackle of laughter at the end of this, he said:

"So I was right in my guess! You are here now as appren-tice in my work for the king." He blinked at me from eyes that ran with the rheumy tears of old age. "And maybe also as my successor?"

I nodded, feeling pity for those tears as I did so, and told him, "But before I start my studies with you, Brother Anselm, I have another commission—which is to take to the Black Douglas all news of the king, and also greetings from him."

The blinking, rheumy eyes became suddenly fixed and shrewd. "In that case, my young friend, you can also carry to the Douglas a most important message from me. But first go and stable your pony." With a dismissive wave of his hand, he turned from me. "The Douglas is almost three days' ride east of here, at the border town of Peebles. And so you can have supper and a bed before riding on your way to him."

I went out to attend to Storm. I ate of the thin fare that was all the friary ever provided. I listened to Brother Anselm outlining my route to Peebles—an easy matter for him, since our journey together into England had already taught him that I possessed what he had referred to then as "a bump of location."

No matter where I am, indeed—as I had already proved in Moray—I can always tell which direction is north. And so the only thing that troubled me during my ride to Peebles was that this took me mostly over wild moorland where the lonely cries of the curlew bird sometimes sent shivers up my back.

That was a small matter, however, compared to the danger of arrest by English soldiers patrolling less-deserted terrain. And indeed, it was not till I was riding upstream of the River

Tweed and almost within sight of the Douglas camp at Peebles that I *was* arrested.

I heard the shouted challenge of *"Qui va là!"*—saw the two horsemen bearing down on me—and then I recognized the face of the one in the lead. I held my hands in the air and called frantically:

"Dalgleish! Andrew Dalgleish!"

He drew rein, and both then came on at a slower pace. I shouted, "Do you not know me, Drew? I marched alongside you at the battle of Buchan Hill!"

He pulled up level with me, peered into my face, and said wonderingly, "God's blood! Crawford—young Martin Crawford. And here was I thinking we had come on some lone Englishman just asking to be split in two!"

I laughed aloud at this, but more from relief than for any other reason. And quickly on this, in case of similar challenges, I asked him to escort me personally to the Douglas himself.

"Most willingly!" Leaving the other man to continue on guard duty, Dalgleish led me on—grinning still at his own joke as he did so and proudly pointing out the burnt-out ruin of the castle beside the camp ahead of us.

"You see that?" he demanded. "You see how far east we've raided now? Peebles Castle, that was. Garrisoned till last week by the English. And the Douglas was supposed to be left just holding our position in the southwest—was he not? As if . . ." He paused to give a spit of contempt. "As if that would content the kind of man *he* is!"

With even greater relish, then, he went on to tell me of

how—as well as managing to keep the southwest under control—the Douglas had been making himself so strongly felt also in the south and southeast. Where he could not manage to capture a castle, it seemed, he simply harried the patrols its commander sent out—harried them so fiercely, in fact, that they became afraid, eventually, to venture out at all.

"Indeed," Dalgleish boasted, "they have even made a song about that—one that their wives sing to hush their bairns to sleep." And hoarsely then, with mock tenderness, he sang,

"Hush thee, hush thee, do not fret thee,
The Black Douglas will not get thee."

In a burst of laughter at the end of this, he left me at the open flap of his commander's tent and rode off, once again hoarsely singing. I heard from within the tent the voice that bade me enter, and so met again at last with the subject of the song.

He had not changed, I saw, except that he was even leaner than before. His greeting to me was pleasant, but brief and to the point. I took my cue from this and was just as brief with him, first over my commission from the king, and next in my delivery of the message from the friar.

"King Edward the Second of England," I told him then, "is in France for his marriage to the French king's daughter, and has meantime left the government of his country in the hands of his favorite courtier, Piers Gaveston. But this Gaveston is an upstart fellow, detested by all the nobility of

129

England. And so now they are all at war over who should rule there instead of him—all of which information is also being sent meanwhile from the black friar to our king."

The Douglas nodded. "So that he will know from it what I now know—that the war between these English nobles will mean that, for the coming summer at least, we can count ourselves free from any further attempt at invasion."

"Yes, sir. Which, of course, will be a great relief not only to you, but even more so to the king in his plans for that summer."

"And these plans are?"

I shrugged. "As to that, sir, all I can tell you is the army rumor that, if events in the north go as the king has planned, he will then turn west to attack Buchan's only remaining ally—his kinsman, John of Lorn. But what that attack would achieve I cannot even begin to guess."

"But I can!" Eyes eagerly gleaming, the Douglas leaned towards me. "It is John of Lorn who rules the territory of Clan MacDougall, and that includes the seaports the English need for landing both troops and supplies—troops to quell any least rebellion from the rest of the Highland chiefs, and supplies for all the enemy garrisons in the north. And so, for the Bruce to smash John of Lorn's power would not only allow all those other clan chiefs at last to join us—"

"But would leave us then with only the English themselves to fight!"

Eagerly I interrupted, and smiling at this, the Douglas agreed, "Exactly so. A clear field against them at last." He rose, then, and clapped me on the shoulder. "The war is moving on, Martin, and moving in our favor!" And it was on this happy note that I left him, to ride back to Brother Anselm.

He was waiting for me, his plans all ready. On the desk in his study were a number of wax tablets with names scratched on the wax. There were also maps of Scotland lying unrolled, one of these showing the position of every castle, another showing the position of every town and abbey.

"These names"—he pointed from one tablet to another— "they are those of my principal informants—the very number of which will tell you how ripe for rebellion the people now are. You will memorize all of them, and then erase them from the wax. And these maps—"

He paused there to flatten the maps with his hands before continuing, "I have prepared these for the sole purpose of passing on to you all the knowledge of the country I have acquired throughout my own travels. But all that knowledge you must now also memorize, because, if you are arrested as a spy, nothing of that kind must ever be discovered on you."

To commit all that information to memory! But the campaign in Moray, I reasoned, had at least given me some practice in conning a map. Besides which, I now had months to study instead of the few hours I had been given then, and my memory had always been a good one.

"As for how you avoid arrest," the friar continued, "the first step in that is for you to acquire a new identity."

I looked in astonishment at him. "And how, pray, do I do that?"

"Quite simply. You will pass yourself off, wherever you go, as a young scholar seeking quiet to pursue your studies— perhaps in some corner in an abbey, where you will always gladly be given shelter. Or perhaps even in a castle—"

"A castle!" In alarm now, instead of astonishment, I interrupted. "But all the castles are occupied by the English."

"Ah, yes. But in all the important ones the governor always keeps his own priest as father confessor. And if you applied to speak to that priest—say on some knotty point of Latin grammar—who knows what you might discover about the castle's defenses."

I glanced again at the maps, realizing fully now why they showed the situations of all those abbeys and castles. But to find myself trapped in one of those castles, with only my own wits to save me being found out as a spy . . . With an effort of will to put this thought behind me, I asked:

"And the towns, Brother Anselm? What if I am at a loss to find any of your informants there. What will I do then?"

"You will seek out the Dean of Guild—the official who regulates all the trade in the town—and you will give him a password. If he recognizes it, as most of these officials will, he will give you whatever information he has."

"And that password is—?"

"The same as I gave our young recruit from Nithsdale— you remember him? *Brother Anselm sent me.*"

"But what if some Dean of Guild does not recognize the password? What then?"

"You simply add to it that you are one of my students. He

will then be pleased to think he is gaining grace by finding you shelter in the travelers' hospice that every town provides—but where there is always also at least some information to be gleaned!"

I nodded in acknowledgment of all this, and settled to make a proper study of the names on the wax tablets and then of the maps. Brother Anselm leaned over my shoulder and approved:

"Good, that is the way to do it. Study the names first, then relate them to the places on the map. And when you come to the map itself, do not forget that you must note not only place names. You must also trace every road, every track between one place and another, and then connect that to your knowledge of where all these various rivers are bridged."

With the same finger-stabbing gesture that Bishop David had used, he moved his hand from south to north up the map in front of me. "Tweed, Forth, Tay, Dee, Don, Spey," he recited, and added, "There, Martin. There is a good rhyme to remind you of the names of those rivers!"

"A children's rhyme!" I scoffed. "I do not need such to remind me."

"I hope not," he said, and something in his tone then made me look up to see a face that had suddenly become very serious.

"I hope not," he repeated, "because remember this also, Martin. Your role as wandering scholar means that, except for the knife you may need to cut your food, you must go unarmed."

He put a hand on my shoulder as he spoke, and the anxiety on his face was so obvious that I felt forced to try to take the edge off his concern.

"Cut my food," I mocked. "As if I am likely to get anything solid enough to need cutting!"

I had my reward for this—a half smile of relief on his wrinkled old face. But that, for the next few months, when I daily crammed knowledge into my head, and he nightly examined me on all I had studied, was the last smile I had from him. He did admit, all the same, that I was an apt pupil. And gradually, too, as his informants brought word of happenings in the north of the country, the atmosphere between us became more and more cheerful.

"The Earl of Buchan is fled into England. In Buchan itself not one stone remains standing on another!"

That was the news brought in at the end of March by the captain of the *Bonny Lass*, a coastal trader docking at Ayr on its return from Aberdeen, the principal port city of the northeast.

"Bruce is on the move again. All Moray is now his."

That, around the end of April, was the news that filtered down drove roads leading south from Moray, and along the same routes a few weeks later came word that the king was busily storming all the English-held castles lying inland of the city of Aberdeen. At the same time, too, came word from the Black Douglas that the king had sent the lord Edward to help him in tightening the grip he had already gained on the southeast.

"Aberdeen has fallen to the Bruce! He has captured its castle and has ridden in to the acclaim of all its citizens."

It was near the end of June that this happened, the news of it again brought by sea. But in the last week of July came a very different kind of message, delivered this time by a journeyman silversmith who had traveled from Inverness to seek work in Ayr.

"Martin," the friar told me then, "the king is to hold a war conference in Inverness. He commands that the Black Douglas should immediately attend him there, and commands also that you should go with the Douglas."

Chapter Eleven

The conference took place in the Town House of Inverness, with all the senior officers of our army crowded expectantly in there. The Douglas found us a place beside his longtime friend Sir Thomas Randolph, nephew of the king. The king himself rose to address us, and had spoken no more than a few sentences when the whole room burst out into excited comment.

It was to happen at last—that long-rumored attack on the very last of Buchan's allies, John of Lorn! The king held up a hand for silence, and warningly went on:

"But hear this. We can and will achieve a great victory over John of Lorn, and presently, I shall tell you how. But even so, that will still not prevent him trying to regroup his scattered forces at his castle of Dunstaffnage. The capture of that castle must therefore follow immediately on his defeat in battle. Yet Dunstaffnage is so strongly built that it cannot be taken except by a long siege. Or else by trickery. And for that, I shall need a volunteer."

Hands shot up from all around the room—a forest of hands that included even that of his page, our one-time hostage, Sir Walter of Ross, as well as that of his squire, de Picard. But no. With a shake of his head first towards the boy and then to the rest of us, the Bruce explained:

"My lords, gentlemen, my volunteer must be a young man who can ride hard and very fast, but who is still recognizably not a soldier." He paused there at the murmur of disappointment running around the room. And then, as all the hands dropped down to leave one only still held aloft, he added, "Furthermore, since the only language spoken in the MacDougalls' territory is their native Gaelic, my volunteer must also be a Gaelic speaker."

That last hand belonged to de Picard—and he spoke no Gaelic. As his hand, too, dropped down, I saw the king's gaze fixed on me, and knew at last that I was right in my guess over his reason for summoning me to that conference.

I was the only one there who answered to all the requirements he had named. I was young. I had a swift mount and had proved I could ride hard. I was not a soldier. Like the Bruce himself, I had been born and bred in Carrick, and like him, too, therefore, I had the Gaelic spoken there. But I had not volunteered—and he knew why! I met his gaze squarely, and said:

"One question, Sire. Will I have to kill anyone?"

"Martin!" He shook his head at me. "That was not in the agreement I made with you. You will recognizably not be a soldier simply *because* you will carry no weapons—if, that is, you are indeed willing to volunteer."

They were all waiting for me to answer—all that roomful of officers waiting to see just what stuff I was made of. But even more importantly, there was that vow I had made. I put hesitation behind me, and said:

"I am willing, Sire."

He nodded. "Good! I will give you your orders presently. But meanwhile, for all of you here, this is my plan for defeating John of Lorn."

It was like every other plan I had known him to make— a simple one, yet still brilliant in its very simplicity.

"We cannot enter Lorn's territory," he told us, "except by way of a mountain pass so narrow that he is bound to ambush us there. But we shall be ready for that—more than ready."

Rapidly but clearly then he sketched out his plan for a counterambush, and finished this by calling the Douglas to speak to him. Heads bent in quiet talk, the two of them stood together for a few minutes. The Douglas left him to rejoin the excited discussion that had meanwhile been going on among his fellow officers, and it was then that the king called me to him.

"For the beginning of your part in this," he told me, "you will be under the command of the Douglas. And only when he says 'Go!' will you go to do as I tell you now."

Carefully, and in great detail then, he described what I had to do. I listened, with my mind once more filled with the same mixture of dread and excitement I had felt before my one and only meeting with old Longshanks, and a week later we marched against John of Lorn.

* * *

The first part of our route took us down the Great Glen—almost four thousand of us marching to the sound of bagpipes skirling a war rant that would certainly add to the warnings that John of Lorn must already have heard about us.

The men stepped lightly to the sound of that bagpipe tune. But with three days' march ahead of us, our progress soon settled down to a steady plod that took us first to Spean Bridge, then due east for six miles to Roy Bridge. From there we started the long southward march over the bleak moor that now lay between us and Glen Orchy—the glen leading directly into John of Lorn's territory.

On our third day we marched southwest down Glen Orchy, to camp that night near the village of Dalmally. I ate my share of our usual oatmeal mixed with cold water. I made my way over to the king and found that, as arranged, our scouts had reported to him there.

"There will be no change in orders for you," he told me. "The scouts all agree in their reports. John of Lorn has summoned every available man against us. And so, just as I thought would be the case, Dunstaffnage has been left with only doorkeepers to guard it."

I looked then for the archers under the command of the Black Douglas, and found he had ordered them to camp in woodland well away from the meadow that held the main body of our army. An essential precaution, I thought, Dalmally being so near to MacDougall territory. Also, there were a thousand of these archers. And with no true dark in the Highlands in summer, the Douglas would need the cover of that wood-land when the time came that night to secretly withdraw them from the rest of our force.

I led Storm through the trees till I found the Douglas him-self, wrapped in his plaid and already lying down. I muffled Storm's hooves as I had been told to do. I wrapped myself up as he had done and lay down beside him. But not to sleep.

I had Storm's reins held lightly in one hand as I lay there waiting for the signal from the Douglas. Yet still, as I did so, I heard in my mind the sound of another voice—that of the king explaining to his officers:

"The pass that leads into John of Lorn's territory is guarded by the mountain called Ben Cruachan, and the pass itself is called the Pass of Brandir. On one side of this pass— the right-hand side coming from our direction—the foot of Ben Cruachan drops down in steep cliffs. On the other side— the left—there is another sharp drop to the deep waters of Loch Awe. The space between cliffs and loch, also, is so narrow that it gives hardly room at some points for two men to ride abreast. And so, as I have already warned, it is in this Pass of Brandir that John of Lorn is bound to set ambush for us."

"Are you ready?" The reality of the Douglas's voice whis-pering in my ear brought me jerking upright. All around me, through the shadowy forms of the trees, I saw other shadowy forms—those of men also raising themselves from the ground. I left my plaid lying where it fell lest it encumber me in the dash I would have to make to Dunstaffnage. And with Storm on her muffled hooves plodding soundless beside me, I followed the archers creeping free of their woodland shelter.

From the more-or-less level ground of the surrounding meadows, we made the wide sweep needed to reach the shoulder of Ben Cruachan. The foothills rising to that shoulder loomed before us. We climbed these quickly, yet still—as we had been commanded—without even the sound of loose rock dislodged to betray our presence there, and arrived at last on the ridge for which we had aimed.

In a whisper, then, the Douglas instructed me how to begin following the further directions I had been given. The ridge, he pointed out, continued to run along the side of the mountain for some considerable distance to our right before it spread out eventually into grass and rock sloping easily down towards the floor of the pass below us.

"And once you have got as far as that," he finished, "you will be well past the scene of the action that will happen here. But ride fast, all the same, just as you were told to do."

I settled down then, as the others had already done, and saw that our position had placed us facing towards Loch Awe at the foot of the mountain. I saw, too, that our ridge sloped slightly upwards at its outer edge, thus making it like a sort of parapet that hid the presence of our archers both from anyone on the loch or in the pass below us.

A glance at the sky showed that this still had the grayish white of nighttime. Below and in front of us, the waters of Loch Awe heaved a darker gray. There was little to be seen, in fact, and nothing at all to betray the enemy force that the

Bruce had reckoned was bound to be lying in ambush somewhere below our ridge.

We waited, the archers with their bows strung, their
arrows at the ready; and gradually the grayish white turned
to the white light that always comes just before dawn. Then,
in primrose yellow and rose red, came the trembling glory of
dawn itself, and at last the first sight of the sun's rim to draw
fugitive darts of gold from the sullen heave of the loch's
waters.

We were not far up the side of the mountain, I realized
then. Just as planned, in fact, we were well within bowshot of
the floor of the pass. We waited, no sound of any kind among
us. The sun rose higher, high enough to lay a trail of gold
along the loch. A black object appeared on that trail—a boat
of some kind. It was traveling west to east, drawing closer all
the time to the loch's nearer shore, close enough at last for the
man beside me to identify it.

"A galley!" he whispered. "One of John of Lorn's galleys!"
The galley kept on its course till it was close enough to the
pass to view everything that might be intended to happen
there—close enough for the man beside me again to whisper,
"And there's Lorn himself aboard it!"

I peered towards the figure standing on the galley's deck,
and saw that—whether or not he was John of Lorn—he was
certainly wearing on his cap the eagle feathers that only a
chief was entitled to wear. A sound caught my ear, a familiar
sound—that of marching feet. Our army, at last, was advancing along the pass, advancing towards its narrowest part. The

sound grew rapidly louder. I dared to peer over the parapet, and saw the first of the army's vanguard of Highlanders.

They were keeping close formation, and marching rapidly. Brave men, I thought. Brave men, knowing they were marching straight into an ambush! Yet still they came on until it seemed that, in no time at all, the whole of that narrowest stretch of the pass was crammed with them. And then it happened. The ambush was sprung—from somewhere below our ridge, and with the same tactics as the Bruce had used at Buchan Hill.

A hail of rocks came hurtling down on the Highlanders— but they were no hapless English force unsuspecting of this tactic, and the stones were nowhere near the size of the boulders hurled there. It was not for nothing, either, that all of our Highlanders carried shields—"targes," as they called these— made of bullhide and patterned with great studs of brass. As one man they swung these targes up over their heads, and that hail of rocks bounced harmlessly away from hundreds of surfaces as unyielding as steel.

The stone throwing finished as suddenly as it had started, but was followed immediately by armed men bursting out from behind every boulder, every clump of heather at the side of the track, and from every crevice in the cliff below us. Swords flashed, axes swung as these men closed with our own, and ringing out through the clamor came the voice of the Douglas ordering:

"Arrows ready!"

Our archers, a front rank kneeling, a back rank standing,

fitted arrows to their bows. The Douglas pointed up the pass to our right, to a horde of MacDougall men sweeping down to reinforce those of their men already engaged with ours.

"Arrows away!" The Douglas roared again as he pointed. And like some fierce black wind suddenly made visible, a thousand arrows went whistling down on this MacDougall reinforcement. Again, and again, and again, that black wind struck with the twang of a thousand bowstrings released, the whine of a thousand arrows flying out beyond the heads of our own men to find their targets in that further enemy force.

The Bruce plan, once again, had worked. The ambushers had been ambushed!

The cloth I had used to muffle any sound from Storm as we secretly climbed to our ridge was still around her hooves. I bent to whip this away, and straightened to hear the voice of the Douglas in my ear:

"Go, Martin!" he was yelling. "The bridge—make for the bridge *now!*"

I jumped for the saddle. I urged Storm forward, blessing the sureness of foot that took us both safely along the way the Douglas had pointed out to me. The sounds of battle from below grew less and less the nearer I drew to the point where the mountain ridge petered out into the slope of grass and rock he had described. And there, leading away from this slope, was once again the track through the pass, but with the River Awe now to the left of this.

I rode hard until I came to the bridge that spanned this river. It was made of wood, I found, and I had already been warned that the thirty-foot length of it was an essential link in the only track leading to Dunstaffnage. I sent Storm clattering over it, and at the edge of the woodland on its farther side, I settled myself to wait as I had been told I must do then.

No sound from the pass reached my hiding place, however much I strained to hear. I was too far away by then from the battle to make that possible. And so, instead of useless wondering on how that might be going for us, I thought instead of Dunstaffnage and tried to prepare my mind for what I had to do there.

That castle, I knew, was a massive tower in the shape of a square with a circular tower abutting from each corner of the square. And there was only one entrance to it—the door I would have to trick the castle guards into opening. I gripped more closely to the tree trunk I was holding. It had not been too hard at the time, to volunteer for that. But this, the waiting for action, this *was* hard.

Again and again I peered through the flickering green of the undergrowth in front of me, and found at last that my prayer for the waiting to be over was being answered. The sounds I had been straining to hear became shouts—drawing nearer, always nearer. Figures appeared on the moor beyond the far side of the river—a wild-yelling band of MacDougalls racing towards the bridge. They were holding axes aloft as they ran, and being pursued by some of our own men.

The MacDougalls reached the bridge; but instead of fleeing across it, they began to hack away at its supports, their axes coming down in hasty thuds against the wood. And that,

I realized, could mean only one thing. They must have been defeated in the pass. And yet, if they destroyed that bridge, then made a stand here beside the river, they could still manage to stop our men from reaching Dunstaffnage.

An arrow took one of the MacDougall axemen in the back—then another, and another. Their bodies fell splashing into the river and were swept swiftly past my hiding place. I looked up from this to see the rest of those axemen now grappling fiercely with the Bruce soldiers who had pursued them, and within seconds of that to see also that the moor had become the scene of a running battle between MacDougall and Bruce men, all with the bridge as their goal.

Horses loomed suddenly into my view—our cavalry beginning to cut a way through the chaos on the moor. Some more of the Bruce men gained the bridge and held position on it. I saw my brother, Sean, among these, coolly directing their action. Sean was an officer now, and well used to ordering others.

I saw yet more Bruce men—many more of them—racing across the bridge to gain a vantage position on the far bank of the river. They lined up there waiting for the MacDougalls who had plunged into the river with the idea of gaining that same position.

Swords and axes swung at these MacDougalls trying to struggle up onto the far bank; spears thrust down at them. I looked away from the mangled bodies beginning to float past me, away from the gouts of bright blood spurting into the brawling brown of the river. There were MacDougalls now

146

fleeing in all directions over the moor, and our cavalry was very near. It was a small force—only seventy, which was all we had at the time—but still sufficient for our purpose. And there was the king in their lead when, at last, they gained the bridge.

I was in the saddle by the time he had thundered across it. I fell into place alongside him, my little Storm gamely keeping up with the pace of his larger beast. And like this, with the rest of the troop following close behind, we continued on the track to Dunstaffnage.

It dipped and wound, and dipped and wound again, that track. It was so rough, too, that we had to drop our pace to a trot, and it was only then that I had the chance to ask the king what he thought the final outcome of the battle would be.

"Total defeat for John of Lorn." Briefly at first he answered me, and then went on to say, "His men could not hold us in the pass—not after the number they lost to our archers. And you must have seen for yourself their failure to regroup at the bridge. The MacDougalls, Martin, are a spent force."

But not, I thought, if I failed in my task at Dunstaffnage! Because it was there, in an absolutely impregnable fortress, that they *could* succeed in regrouping.

With Loch Etive now sliding by on our right, we bore steadily on. Etive turned to run into Loch Linnhe, the great sea loch overlooked by Dunstaffnage. We reached the point where the track fell away into a steep wooded slope leading down to the castle, and leaving our mounts hidden there, we worked our way down this slope.

The trees petered out into shrub. We dropped to hands and knees to crawl through this lesser cover, careful as we did so not to shake the bushes and so rouse suspicion among the lookouts on duty somewhere high on the castle walls. We came almost to the end of the shrub before the king signaled a halt and turned to ask me:

"Ready, Martin?" I nodded, and showed him the wedge of wood I had kept all that day stuffed inside my jacket. He squinted upwards to where we could now see the figure of a lookout outlined dark against the blueness of the sky. "Remember, then," he said, "as soon as you have tricked them into opening that door, we will be there behind you. And so go now—and God go with you!"

I rose to my feet, thrust roughly through the remainder of the scrub, and broke into a staggering run towards the castle. I held my right arm across my chest as I did so, to give the impression that it had been broken and needed support. I also called out loudly in the Gaelic, and waved upwards to the lookout with my left arm.

The lookout began waving in reply, then vanished from his post. I staggered on, fervently hoping that he had seen what he had been intended to see—a figure who looked and sounded like a local herd boy who had got himself into trouble of some kind.

The huge bulk of the castle loomed above me. The entrance to it, that sole entrance, was in its south tower. I began staggering towards that tower, still crying out as if for help.

I reached the tower, and with one foot on the curving flight of stone steps built onto it, I heard voices coming from behind the door at the top of the steps.

The door was in two leaves massively constructed of wood covered with iron studs. A crack appeared where the two leaves met at the door's center. I staggered farther up the steps, and the crack between the leaves became wider, the voices behind the crack grew louder. Were there ten men, twenty men, inside that castle? Or had our scouts' report been wrong, and it would be something more like two hundred against our seventy?

I staggered on towards the door, still in my role of wounded herd boy. Yet still that door was slow to open, and I guessed then at the sheer weight of those two massive leaves making it hard for the guards to pull them apart. But once a push from outside was added to that pull from inside . . .

I barged against the opening, thrusting with all the force I could muster. And then, with the pretence of simply having fallen against it out of sheer weakness, I collapsed beside one of the leaves now swinging smoothly backwards. A dozen or so of armed men came crowding around me, all talking at once, all throwing questions at me. I lay prone, gasping out my prepared story—that of the herd boy unfortunate enough to have been caught up in the fighting at the Pass of Brandir, and seeking help now for the wound suffered there.

Rambling and stuttering, I got this out to them, all the time using my prone position to disguise the fact that I was pushing my wooden wedge more and more firmly beneath

149

the leaf of door beside me. The men began helping me to rise—but I had already made time enough for the Bruce and his men to dash to the castle. And it would take several blows of a hammer now to dislodge that wedge!

I thrust aside the helping hands and scrambled to my feet. Muscles tensed for the effort, I made a leap away from the open door, and then a second leap that took me halfway down the steps. Shouts of surprise echoed behind me. There was a parapet on either side of the steps, and from beyond the parapet on my left I heard other shouts. I vaulted over this parapet, and landed just ahead of the men racing towards the steps.

Our men, Bruce's men! And I had successfully pulled off for them the trick that would let them take the castle. I stayed where I had landed, sitting with my head down on my knees, my mouth open on great breaths of relief. It would be only minutes now before Dunstaffnage was in our hands, and— just as I had exclaimed once to the Douglas—we would be left at last with only the English to fight!

PART III

The Lion Rampant

Chapter Twelve

We were on our way to the convent that held our little sister, Sean and I—the first time we had really met in the four years since the capture of Dunstaffnage had brought the Bruce's northern campaign to its successful end.

Sean, in the course of that four years, had taken part in all the fighting that had driven the English out of almost the whole of the rest of the country, and was still as bloodthirsty as ever against them. He was just as condescending to me, too, in the way he spoke, almost his first words being to jeer at my pony.

"A bad choice, that," said he, nodding towards him. "He bites—or so I have heard."

The pony was the black that my gillie friend, Ewen, had ridden at Barra Hill. "Snapper" I had called him, because of that bad habit of biting. But I had cured him of that habit, and he was fast, almost as fast as my little Storm. . . .

I rode on, ignoring his jeer and seeing nothing of the

countryside around me, my thoughts once more suddenly brimming with the guilt I had always felt over Storm's death.

"He's a spy! After him!"

Once again in my mind I heard the voice of the archer who had found me prying around the battlements of Roxburgh Castle. Once again I relived the moment when, instead of trying to talk my way out of danger, I had bolted and then relied on Storm's speed to carry me out of arrow range. And it had been she, instead, who had taken that arrow in her gallant little heart!

Vaguely, I became aware of Sean's voice continuing over my silence, yet still I could not now help pursuing other memories of the four years since Brother Anselm had taught me the craft of a spy—the nights spent in reconnaissance of an English strong point, the careful feeling of my way through the talk of English soldiers in one strange inn after another, the many secret conversations with those on my list of informants. And what of that ride from the English town of York, that long and hard ride to warn the king of Edward the Second's latest attempt to invade our country . . .

Sean's voice, speaking of that same invasion, jerked my attention back to him. He was quoting the king's orders for resisting it, I realized, reciting the very words the king had used to his army.

"We must make the country itself fight for us. We know its bogs, its hills, its mists, its moors. The English commanders do not. We know where to find supplies. They do not—and their lines of communication are already far stretched."

154

"That," Sean added, "was what he told us all. And so we did as he ordered then—retreated before their forces, retreated into wild and ever wilder terrain, always leaving only scorched earth behind us, always leading them further astray, always making sure they grew ever more hungry. And then, each time we had put them at a loss on how to come to grips with us, that was when we struck at them—and then made off again, as swiftly as we had come!"

So leaving a thoroughly demoralized army with nothing to do, finally, except to retreat to their own land! Silently, thinking then of the way I had followed that retreat and reported back on it to the king, I added my own tailpiece to the story. But Sean was turning towards me now, smiling, obviously expecting compliments on his own part in all this. I duly paid these to him, and condescendingly then, he asked:

"And you, little brother? What have you now to tell me about your adventures?"

My adventures? I thought rapidly. Sean was my only kin now, apart from our poor, mad little sister, and so what right had I to keep secrets from him? But Sean, on the other hand, had all the curiosity of most other talkative people, and if I spoke at all of my many hair's-breadth escapes over the past four years, he was bound to want to hear more. Unlike myself, too, Sean had never learned to guard his tongue, and my whole value to the king now was the secrecy my role demanded.

"Well?" He was becoming impatient for me to answer, and there was now in his tone the kind of laughing sneer he had so often before directed at me. "You are still with the army, I know, but what *have* you been doing since that day at Dunstaffnage Castle—the day you set out, singlehanded, to capture it for us?"

So that was how he had chosen to look on what I had done then! Rage swept over me, confusing my mind even further. And then, through the blur of thoughts there, I heard his voice continuing:

"But you have book learning, of course. And so, I suppose, you are now just some sort of clerk?"

Some sort of clerk!

I grabbed at the phrase. The king had a country to govern now as well as having to continue his struggle against those that were left of the invaders. He had sheriffs to appoint in all the recovered territories—and had I not helped to pen the letters of authority to those sheriffs? I turned to Sean, glad to have found something that would fob him off at the same time as it gave me a chance to vent my anger.

"And pray tell me," I demanded, "why should you presume to sneer at me for a clerk? Is it just that you are ignorant of the way things have changed since you and I first joined the king? Because, if that *is* the reason, it is high time you learned that these past four years have given him much more to do than simply wielding a sword. And so for me to act as clerk to any of the officials he now needs makes me every bit as useful to him as you or any other of his soldiers!"

"Heugh!" Sean gave the kind of whistling sigh that had always been his response when I tried to retaliate against any of his gibes at me. "So the little brother has some stuff in him after all, eh?" And with anger flaring again in me at this, I retorted:

"Pray less, please, of this 'little' brother. I am near twenty-one years now, after all—as Morag, if only she were here to do so, would doubtless also remind you."

That sobered Sean. But the unkindness of the cut I had dealt him also sobered me. Because, I knew, he had loved Morag in his own way as much as I had loved her in mine.

I rode alongside him for a while in a silence that matched his own, until conscience at last forced me into encouraging him to talk again.

"That story you were telling," I said, "the story about the lord Edward and his fifty against fifteen hundred—what finally happened there?"

Sean turned his lean, scarred face towards me, his eyes once again suddenly alight with interest. "Ah, yes!" he exclaimed. And went on from there with his tale about being one of a scratch force of fifty, mounted on baggage ponies by the lord Edward, and taking advantage of a thick mist to trail this English force of fifteen hundred.

"And then," he continued, "when the mist became so thick that they could see no more than an arm's length ahead, we charged them—bursting through their column first from their right flank, then from their left. And charged them again, and again, each time at a different point in their column, each time on the opposite flank to the one before. We yelled, too, as we charged—yelled like all the demons of hell. And oh God,

157

you should have seen the heads that rolled each time, the blood that spurted!"

Why had I encouraged him to tell such a story! "Sean! Please Sean—" I began.

But his voice bore over mine, a loud excited voice saying, "And between each of our charges, of course, the further tactic was to keep ourselves hidden in the mist—all of which led them to suppose they must be under attack from some huge body of cavalry. And believe me, you should have seen, too, the panic this caused among them!"

"Which meant in the end, I suppose, that they broke and scattered before you?" I spoke quickly, hoping to bring the story as soon as possible to its end.

"They did!" Grinning widely now with satisfaction, Sean nodded agreement before he challenged, "And so what have you to say to all that?"

"Only this, Sean." Speaking very quietly, I answered. "Please, when we see Shona, do *not* tell any such tales to her."

"Eh?" He looked blankly at me for a moment, and then spluttered, "You—you— Are you daring to tell me how to talk to my own sister?"

"Yes. Because she is my sister too. One who has had enough of blood and terror and death already in her life. And if she has not yet recovered from what that did to her, if she hears more of such matters from you . . ."

I left my reply unfinished. We had drawn rein, both of us, during this interchange, and his gaze had now locked in mine. There was hostility at first in his. And then, as understanding gradually dawned on him, he looked away and mumbled:

"I know—I think I know what you mean. And I—" He faced me again, his own features quivering with the feeling he was trying to express, but managed at last to finish, "And I promise you now. No words of mine will *ever* deal hurt to Shona."

For once in our lives, I thought then, we had understood one another. Sean had grasped that I was something more than the soft, bookish person he had always taken me to be. I had accepted that he was not so unimaginative as I had always thought him. I nodded acknowledgment of what he had said about Shona. And with an exchange of smiles that completed the release of tension between us, we rode on towards the convent.

She came towards us in the small room set aside there for visitors and immediately took both my hands in hers. But was this really Shona?

I had visited her twice before at the convent—visits that showed her as being still the little girl we had left there all those years ago. And here she was now, tall and slim in a gray gown that covered her from neck to ankles yet still could not quite conceal the grace of her womanly figure. Sean, since we had handed her over to the nuns, had not seen her at all, and he gaped at her even more than I did.

"Shona!" He too, came forward with hands outstretched to grasp hers, but she backed from him. And hurriedly, as if some sixth sense had told her of the kind of story I had

159

warned him not to repeat, she cried out:

"No! No! Your hands have blood on them!"

Sean stared from her to me. His eyes dropped to his hands, still held outstretched. He turned his hands over. The palms were rough. The white lines of healed scars showed on his knuckles, but on neither back nor front of them was there any blood. With another glance at Shona, he bent towards me and whispered:

"Is she still mad, do you think?"

I shook my head. "Wait," I told him. "Just wait." And taking Shona by the hand then, I led her to sit beside me on a bench running along one wall of the room.

"Shona," I asked, "the little princess—the one shut up in a cage in the Tower of London—do you still want her to be freed?"

She nodded to this—very firmly nodded—and told me, "Oh, yes, Martin. I do. I pray for that. Night and day I pray for it—just as I do also for the souls of Mother and Morag."

"Good," I told her. "Good! But you know, do you not, Shona, that the princess cannot be freed until her father, the Bruce, has freed our country? And that he has been given no choice to do that, either, except by war?"

"Yes, I do know all that, Martin. I do. But people get killed in war. And Sean has—"

"Yes, Shona, yes!" Quickly, fearing the distress now in her voice, I interrupted. "I know what you were about to say. But Sean is a soldier. And it is only if he and his kind do their duty as soldiers that the little princess *can* be freed.

And something else I will tell you, Shona, something I know well but have never before spoken of to anyone."

Lifting her chin with the tip of one finger so that she had to look straight at me, I went on, "For more than a year, I was page to the Bruce. And every night before he slept, I saw and heard him at his prayers. Among those, too, there was always one asking forgiveness for the deaths of those he had killed, as well as a prayer of intercession for their souls."

Her eyes still fixed trustingly on me, she breathed, "That is true?"

"Yes," I told her, "true as I stand here. Yet the Bruce is also a soldier doing no more than his duty. And so if I were to tell you now that Sean follows him in this as faithfully as he does in other ways . . ."

I paused to hold that wide and trusting gaze a few seconds longer before turning my head towards Sean. He was a natural-born fighter, and so was the Bruce. But Sean still hated the English, and had come to enjoy killing them. The Bruce regretted the death of every man he had killed, and there was no hatred of any kind in him. In these things lay all the difference between them, the difference that Sean would have to bridge—or at least pretend to bridge—if our sister were not forever to be lost to him.

I held the gaze that met my own. Sean's face, when I had first turned to him, had been sullen. But now, thank God, he was beginning to laugh his usual blustering laugh.

"Would that change your mind about me, Shona?" he asked. "Because Martin is clever, is he not? And it is Martin,

161

of course, who has the right of it now."

Sean was playing up to me. Sean had grabbed the life-line I had thrown him! I watched Shona searching his face, searching with eyes too innocent to realize the falsity of the laughter lines on it. I held my breath till she rose to place both her hands in his, and say softly:

"Sean!"

He drew her towards himself. Nor did she flinch when his arms went round her. To my relief, indeed, she returned his embrace. And when they broke apart again, I was all the more relieved to hear her laugh when he teased:

"But of course, Shona, you always were a silly little goose!"

I jumped to my feet. Pretense or not, Sean was certainly now doing his best to make Shona believe everything I had implied about him was true. And certainly, also, that was enough to put all three of us back onto the footing that used to exist between us. Briskly I said:

"The very same opinion he has always had of me, Shona. But he is still a good enough brother, is he not? And so come along, now, tell us all about yourself—because he is as anxious to hear that as I am."

She spoke to both of us then, eagerly and at length, telling us all about her life in the convent, how kind the nuns were to her, how well they had taught her to nurse the sick, to embroider holy vestments, how happy she was—because of Mother and Morag and the little princess, she explained—to join in all their prayers.

Yet still, young woman as she now was, her way of regarding all she spoke of seemed to us as childish as ever. And when we left her at last waving to us from the convent's gate, Sean asked worriedly:

"What do you say, Martin? *Is* she still mad?"

I shook my head. "No, not what people usually call mad, because—"

I paused there, realizing that Sean could know nothing of the great hospital built by Augustinian monks close by Soutra Hill—the hospital that overlooked the route so often taken by armies invading from England. But I had been fed and rested often by those monks and knew them to be as skilled in dealing with damaged minds as they were at treating war wounds and diseases of the body. Yet how could I speak of them now without revealing that, with their daily view of all who came over Soutra, they were one of my most valuable sources of information?

Carefully, picking my way through all I had heard them say about their work of healing, I asked, "Have you ever noticed, Sean, what a snail does when it is frightened?"

"Of course!" He stared at me. "It draws right back into its shell."

"And takes a long time to come out again—just as it is with Shona now. Or so it would seem, at least. Because she was safe as a child. Then she was frightened, and so she has drawn back in her mind to that safe time."

"Like a snail into its shell, eh?" Sean frowned over this before he asked, "But will she ever venture out of that?"

"I think so," I told him. "But not until that little princess she thinks of so constantly is freed. Because for her, you see, that will mean the end of the war. And it's only when that happens that she will be able to live at last with all the things that have so frightened her. To think with a grown woman's mind, in effect, as well as having the body of a woman."

"Hmm." Sean took a quick, considering glance at me before he said, "If you can see as clearly as that about Shona, you *are* clever. By God's bones, Martin, you are! But—"

Abruptly he drew rein, forcing me to do likewise. "But," he repeated, "you were too clever by half in the way you managed to get her to accept me. Because I had to pretend to her, had I not? Pretend I am something different from what I am. Pretend that I do not hate those damned English."

I faced him as coolly as I could. "And did that offend you?"

"After what they did to our family! It did offend me. By God, it did! And every blow I have struck since then, let me tell you, has been struck for Mother and for Morag!"

He had shouted his answer at me, and I shouted back at him, "For which neither of them would thank you! And so the sooner you forget this bloodlust you have for the enemy, the sooner also will these two be able to rest in peace!"

"Eh?" His jaw dropping, he stared a moment before he demanded, "But it is only human, is it not, to seek revenge? Just like the Bruce himself, in fact, when he raided Galloway, and killed those who had killed his brothers there."

"The Bruce," I retorted, "is answerable for his own soul—

just as you are answerable for yours. And you heard, did you not, the way I spoke about him to Shona?"

He stared again, his face once more working with an emotion he could not express—something that moved me to take a much quieter tone when I added:

"Think about that, Sean. Think of what I told Shona about him."

Sean looked away, making no answer to this. Nor was there any further exchange between us on the way back to our joint destination—the town of Ayr, where the latest of the king's parliaments had been held. I was aware, all the same, that he was glancing occasionally at me as we rode. And looking back when we had parted there—he to the army encampment beside the River Ayr, I to go into the town, but both of us again without speaking—I saw him holding his mount stock-still while he gazed after me.

Was he considering what I had said to him? I wondered. And supposing he was, would that make him any different from what he had become? I thought of our mother and Morag, of our poor young sister praying peace for their souls, and hoped that it would.

Chapter Thirteen

I t was a bad time for all of us, the year of that visit to Shona—the second year in succession when crops all over the country had failed. We could not buy food from abroad, either, nor could we trade for food—not with the king's war chest now completely empty and English pirate ships blocking all our efforts to trade.

More and more as I rode about the country, I noted that hunger was turning now into famine. And if we could not even live, how could we carry on the fight? I thought of how the Bruce had battled in the past four years to free us bit by bit of English rule. Despairingly I wondered what he could possibly do now—then was shamed into remembering that it was always when our fortunes seemed at their lowest that he had made some new and bold stroke. And that second year of hunger saw his boldest yet.

A new army was assembled at Ayr. I was told of my own small part in his plan. And since I had to ride past the

Dominican friary in any case on the way to carry out my orders, I decided to stop there to let Brother Anselm know what was afoot.

I found him, as I had expected, lying on his pallet bed in the tiny little cell that had for so long been his home—a sick man now, his small body even more shrunken than before, his voice weak. Yet still, his eyes brightened at the sight of me, and his first words were:

"You have brought me news! I see that in your face. And so tell me now—quickly!"

"The king is about to lead an invasion force into England."

"What!" Mouth open in delighted astonishment, the old man shot upright in bed.

I nodded. "It's true, Brother Anselm. We must have food. We must have money to buy from abroad. And so he will turn the tables on the English now by taking the army deep into *their* land, looting cattle and grain, taking prisoners for ransom, seizing valuables of every kind, emptying the treasury of every town he strikes. And he can do all that. There could not be a better time for it, in fact, because—"

I paused to draw enough breath to let me finish this tirade, and snatching my words away from me, the old man echoed:

"Because the English king is once again too much at war with his own barons to prevent him doing so. But tell me more, Martin. Who will be our king's principal captains? What route will he take? And who, while he is gone, will act as Regent here? The lord Edward?"

"No—his nephew, Sir Thomas Randolph, will be Regent, with the lord Edward and the Black Douglas as his captains. As for the route, that will be south till they've passed Carlisle, then they'll march east as far as Durham."

"And your part in all this?"

"The part for which you trained me!" Smiling now at the old man, I went on, "Because, of all the places on that route, Durham is the only one with a castle. And so my orders now are to spy out the likely opposition from its garrison."

"In that case . . ." Brother Anselm leaned forward, ready as always with advice, and it was with all this stored away in my mind that I continued eventually on my way.

My route to Durham was the same one the army would take—south from Ayr to the point where I had seen old Longshanks die, then east to pass Hexham, Corbridge, and Chester-le-Street—all of them the prosperous market towns marked down for attack. A swift ride of only twenty miles from the last of these brought me finally to Durham—or, at least, to the point where Brother Anselm had told me I would have a good view of that city.

I threaded my way through the woodland leading up to that point. And there, at the foot of the slope dropping away from it, lay the River Wear flowing in a long, lazy loop around the city of Durham on its farther side. At the foot of the slope was one of the several bridges across this river. The skyline of the city itself was dominated on the right by its cathedral, and on the left by its castle—both of these built in a sort of yellowish stone. To the castle's left was a big, open market-place. Beyond castle and market on one side, and beyond the cathedral on the other, was the huddle of roofs that made up the rest of the city.

I stood for several minutes imprinting all this on my mind before leading Snapper back through the wood to a clearing that would shelter both of us for the night. I tethered him there to graze and to drink from the stream that ran through the clearing. I ate sparingly of the bread I had brought, plan-ning all the time I ate. And then, with brushwood pulled over me for warmth, I settled down to get such rest as I could.

Dawn saw me wide-awake and already on my way down into the city. I had left Snapper behind me in the clearing, there being no part for him in my plan, the first move in which was to mingle with the beggars waiting for the cathe-dral Almoner to appear with the daily distribution of bread to the poor.

I had gathered information, in the past, from just such a move, beggars always being much given to grumbling, and so I was quick then to join in the complaints over the hardness of the Almoner's charity bread. The beggar beside me was the one who had most to say on this, and with a jerk of my head towards the castle, I added to his complaint:

"Aye, better go for a soldier than take the cathedral's dole. Because—I lay all the money I'll never have—there's better food up there than we'll ever see. And plenty of it too."

The man's mouth opened on a guffaw of laughter that showed teeth as black and broken as rotten fence posts.

169

"Fat pigs!" he said contemptuously, and shot a gobbet of spit through his broken teeth. "With nothing to do all day but eat."

"What—no drill? No marching?"

"You're a stranger, heh?" Broken-teeth looked me up and down. "Aye, by the sound of your voice you must be. Well, stranger, let me tell you now that Durham—rich city as it is— is still no more than a backwater where nothing ever happens. And so what would be the point of drilling and marching for the lazy swine in the castle there?"

The Almoner, I thought, was beginning to look a bit suspiciously at me by then. Maybe because he, too, had noted the Scottish tones in my voice? With quickened memories of other forays into England, and other times when these had been on the point of betraying me, I gave Broken-teeth a wave of farewell before drifting away over the open ground between the cathedral and the castle.

"Check the stables," Brother Anselm had advised. *"That's not only your best but your quickest way to find the strength of their cavalry."* But to check the stables meant first gaining access to the castle itself and then working my way into the confidence of someone there. And that, I knew from past experience, would take time—time I could not afford with the army now well on its way south.

I passed the castle and began sauntering through the marketplace, alive now with stall holders setting up their wares, and richly gowned women followed by servants carrying large baskets. I stopped at the stall of a saddler, where a fat man in

170

a velvet robe was bargaining over the price of a horse bridle. The man in velvet took his leave. The saddler asked politely if he could serve me. I shook my head and said wistfully that his goods were not for the likes of me.

"Too well-made and so too expensive," I added. "Although, of course, with all those *destriers* at the castle, you're bound to do a good trade there."

"*Destriers,*" he echoed. "But those are cavalry horses. And what makes you think—" Abruptly he stopped, his eyes—the keen and clever eyes of a master craftsman—now narrowing the focus of their gaze at me. "I have soldiered in Scotland," he told me. "I know from your voice that you come from there. I know also that your country does not breed *destriers*. And so why should you show interest in them now?"

"Why not?" I asked, and attempted a laugh. "It is human nature, is it not, to envy what one cannot have?"

Was it my fancy, or did his gaze at me narrow even further? I could not tell. Yet still I knew that I needed some confirmation of my guess at what he had suddenly checked himself from telling me—that there were few, if any, *destriers* in the castle stables. I left his stall with my heart beating a little faster than usual, and drifted over to that of a grain merchant.

Casually, I picked up a handful of oats from a sack that lay open there. I rubbed the grains between my hands to separate the chaff from the kernel, then blew away the chaff.

"Good stuff, eh?" the merchant encouraged. I nodded, and said idly, "You'll have good customers for it too, I expect."

With a backward jerk of my head I indicated the castle. "At the castle there."

"There?" The merchant shrugged. "There's not much in the way of oats needed for the kind of beasts *they* have. But for brewers with their heavy dray horses, and carters too . . ." He was turning away from me by then to speak to someone who was obviously a better prospect than I was, but over his shoulder, he shot at me, "Now that *is* a good market."

I walked slowly away from his stall, satisfied now that I had guessed correctly about the lack of *destriers* in the castle stables. And no *destriers* meant no knights in heavy armor. No knights in heavy armor meant that—in one respect, at least—our men would be fighting here on even terms. And so now to discover whatever else I could about those who made up the garrison of the castle.

The cathedral loomed again before me. And there, in the angle where a buttress joined the wall facing the castle, I crouched for the rest of that day with my cap pulled well down to hide my face and my eyes fixed always on the castle gates.

Soldiers passed in and out of those gates. Supply wagons were driven in and out. A few mounted soldiers emerged, but none of these was riding a *destrier*, nor were any such beasts led out for exercise. The guard was changed for another guard. Some of the soldiers came singly, others in groups that made straight for a street where I could see the sign of an inn projecting from a wall.

Most of those I had seen were well-built men, but still with

172

nothing of the lean and hardened look of our own men. And that, at least, did tell me something of the nature of this garrison. It was serving, as Broken-teeth had said, in a backwater where nothing ever happened, and so most of these men had probably never seen active service. Nor did they look fit for that—not with drinking at that inn as their habit!

With the light beginning to fade, I headed for this place as my last possible source of information, and found it to be a dank hole smelling strongly of ale and sweat. But this did at least mean it was not the sort of place where I would risk meeting again the keen eyes of that master saddler. I chose a quiet corner where I could overhear some soldiers talking, and stayed there unnoticed until the door burst suddenly open to admit—of all people—the broken-toothed beggar of that morning.

He was drunk and, like all of his kind in that state, was ready to claim me as a lifelong friend. What was worse, he was slavering over me as his "Scottish friend." The soldiers roared with laughter as I tried to resist his embrace. I struck out in panic at him—to cries of "Shame!" then from the soldiers. But I felt no shame—not when that embrace could have meant death for me. And by the time I had at last fought free of him, I was more than ready to ride back with my report to the king.

The market town of Corbridge was the appointed meeting place. But Corbridge was now no more than a heap of smoking ruins, with the herds of cattle I had earlier noticed in the fields around it swelled to numbers that stretched as far as I could see.

I struggled a way through these to the army encampment, then past a mob of prisoners being held under guard, and finally managed to deliver my report to the king. I had found him conferring with the Black Douglas and the lord Edward, and the moment I finished speaking, he turned to tell these two:

"So you can still take Durham, it seems—even now, with the reduced numbers in your fast force. And Martin . . ." He looked again at me. "I want you with that force so that you can report quickly to me on what happens there."

A fast force? Hurrying along beside the Douglas and the lord Edward to where long columns of men stood lined up and waiting, I begged to be told what this meant.

"It means," said the Douglas shortly, "that the king now needs many of the army as herdsmen to get those cattle back home. He needs guards, too, for his prisoners. And so the rest of us are ordered to press on to the two remaining targets— Chester-le-Street and Durham. And to move fast in that, not burdening ourselves this time with cattle, but taking loot only."

"And prisoners? What about them?"

"We take no prisoners either until we reach Durham. But from the report I heard you give, the pickings there should be rich enough."

I was tired by then, also hungry. I looked around and saw that the Douglas was leading a contingent of Highlanders, and that the lord Edward's force held some of my first friends from the old days in Glen Trool—Alec Farquhar and Hugh Roberton among them.

"I'm famished," I confessed to these two. "My belly thinks my throat's cut."

"You look beat, too," Alec told me, digging a piece of bread from the pouch at his belt, while Hugh added:

"And your pony doesn't look in much better case." He turned from me and singled out the familiar red head of the gillie in charge of those holding a string of baggage ponies. "Ewen," he yelled, "bring one of those beasts over here."

Ewen hurried to obey the call. Quickly, he saddled up the pony to replace Snapper and left me to take my place at the rear of the fast force. We marched off towards Chester-le-Street, and though it was dark by the time we reached there, the attack was still instantly launched. I stayed with the gillies watching the flames that roared up into the night sky; but awesome as it was to witness this, I still could not find it in my heart to pity the citizens waking to these flames.

The king's orders to the army, after all, had been clear. There was to be no random killing. Terror was to be our weapon. Loot was our goal. I could not help but agree, accordingly, when Ewen said:

"Aye, it's one thing for us to be burned out and plundered. They look on that as a matter of course. But they're getting a taste of their own medicine now, eh? And that should maybe teach them."

I went with the gillies as they moved to collect the loot the attack had yielded—gold coins, most of it, along with gold and silver items of all kinds. I helped to load all this into sacks, then to sling the sacks onto the ponies. But even then, it seemed, there was to be no rest for any of us.

The order came to press forward to the attack on Durham—and that was something I *had* to see. I had to see it, moreover, from a position that would let me judge whether or not I had reported correctly on the opposition likely to be met there. And besides—I thought of my woodland view-point, and knew immediately that, rather than march openly on the city, the Douglas would want to take advantage of this.

His contingent was already lining up at the head of our advance, and I spurred hastily forwards to speak to him. He listened closely as I talked and, just as I had expected, grasped instantly the idea that had already occurred to me—that my vantage point would also be the ideal place from which to take the city by surprise.

"Lead the way there," he ordered, and by the time we reached the woodland, he had passed the word along for utter silence throughout the whole army. I led the way to-wards the edge of the woodland. The Douglas joined me there, and together we stood peering down at Durham.

It was well beyond daybreak by then, and life there was in full swing—the beggars gone from the cathedral door, carts full of produce trundling across the bridges to our right, the market crowded with buyers. With one hand going out to unsheathe his sword, the Douglas said grimly:

"Now we will take them properly by surprise!"

He turned, his sword held aloft in the signal to advance.

I pulled hastily aside from the wave of men sweeping forwards in answer to the signal. I saw them take the downward slope to the river at a fast trot, then momentarily lost view of them as the lord Edward's men also swept past me.

The Highlanders following the Douglas gained the bridge leading to the castle and the marketplace. Their pace, as they crossed it, quickened even further. Their voices came exploding upwards to me in the familiar roar of *"BRUCE! BRUCE!"*—a roar that was immediately echoed by the following contingent of the lord Edward's men.

Stalls in the market went flying. Horses reared between their cart shafts. The marketplace itself became a blur of figures running in all directions. Other figures burst from house doors flying suddenly open. The robed figures of monks appeared outside the cathedral and hastily withdrew again, pulling the doors closed behind them.

They would lock and bar these doors, of course, so there was no loot to be gained there. But what of the rest of the city? Where, in all this, were that city's defenders? I stared fixedly at the castle but saw nothing happening there, no gates opening, no soldiers pouring forth in counterattack. Yet still there was house after house now burning. Still there were doors being kicked in, people running and screaming in panic. And still, throughout all this, the castle gates remained obstinately closed.

I found Ewen breathing down my neck, as he and others of the gillies crowded round to follow the direction of my stare.

"The castle!" Ewen exclaimed. "Martin, why are there no

knights in armor charging out from the castle?"

"Because there are none to charge," I told him, and was struck, even as I spoke, by what my words meant for the men of the castle garrison.

Those men—quite unlike our own—could never have been called on to fight without armored and mounted knights ahead to break the force of battle for them. Garrison life, moreover, had been too easy for them. And when they saw all those wild, axe-swinging Highlanders charging across the bridge, when they heard for the first time the bellowing of that Bruce war cry . . .

I found myself laughing aloud at the thought of the terror that must have struck into them. But when the gillies pressed to know the reason for this laughter, Ewen shut them up by saying sharply:

"Leave Martin alone. He has reasons for what he says and does that are none of our concern."

Ewen knew nothing about me except that I was the king's swift rider, but we been friends ever since the night we had crouched together at the top of Loudon Hill. I thanked him with a look, and we sat then in silence until the flames from the town had died sufficiently to let us go about our separate tasks.

It was the space between the castle and the cathedral that had been chosen as the place for the prisoners to be held and for the gillies to collect the loot. I left them to their work while I went to ask directions to the Douglas from Sir Walter of Ross, the officer in charge of the prisoners' guard. He turned from

178

speaking to my old friend Alec Farquhar, causing me almost to step on one of the women prisoners.

She was a big woman, plump, with a long chain of gold links draped round her neck. She thrust her face at me, a face gone as purple as her velvet gown.

"Savages!" she screamed. "That's what you are—savages!"

I jerked my head aside from the spit spraying my cheek. *Savages!* After what *they* had done to *my* family! Between rage at the injustice of the word and sudden remembered grief, I felt the sting of tears that I had always before wept in secret. Blinking, trying hard to regain control of myself, I backed from the woman and blundered straight into the man behind me—Alec's companion of Glen Trool days, Hugh Roberton. He caught me, put me aside, and then harshly challenged her:

"Savages, eh? Yet we do not war against women—not like those that you call your soldiers. And apart from the ransom you will pay"—with one hand reaching out to her gold chain as he spoke, he ripped it from her neck—"that," he finished, "is all that will happen to you. And so who now is the savage?"

The gold chain, as Hugh tossed it contemptuously behind him, was caught by one of the gillies. I heard my name called, and was relieved to see the Douglas approaching. I went to meet him, and pointing to the loot being loaded onto the ponies, he exclaimed:

"No more need for hunger, eh? Not with all this wealth!"

179

"No, sir," I answered absently, my thoughts still bitter over the encounter with the woman prisoner.

"And when you make your report on it," he continued, "add that the lord Edward will bring back the prisoners while I march on to attack the port of Hartlepool."

"Sir? But sir, I cannot speak so to the king, without also telling him why you mean thus to exceed his orders."

"Ships!" With something more like a wolf's grin than his usual pleasant smile, the Douglas answered me. "I mean to scuttle the English pirate ships in port at Hartlepool. Give that as my reason!"

"I will, sir," I told him. And with all my recent self-pity swept away in a sudden wish to show myself as strong in our cause as the Douglas himself, I hurried off with this to add as spice in my report to the king.

Chapter Fourteen

astles!" the king announced, and it was not
hard to guess what he would say next.

Here we were in January of the year following
Durham—the year of Our Lord thirteen hundred
and thirteen. English cities afraid of being raided again were
still paying truce money into our war chest. Trade with coun-
tries abroad was once more smoothly flowing. Their rulers
were friendly to the Bruce cause, so that Bernard de Linton,
Abbot of Arbroath—but also the king's Lord Chancellor—was
constantly receiving envoys who brought to him all the news we
needed about affairs in England. Yet even so, there were still
many of our people being terrorized into paying English taxes—

"—their homes plundered, their lives forfeit to so-called
English justice." Forcefully the king's voice continued my own
train of thought. "All of which is possible only because of the
garrisons in the castles they are still managing to hold. And
it is not until we can recapture all of these that our land will
at last be free."

I waited to learn the outcome of the discussion that broke out then, and was in no way surprised to hear what this was. The English had around eleven garrisons controlling the whole southeast province of Lothian. In the border country, too, they still held Roxburgh Castle. North of Lothian they still held only two castles—Perth and Stirling. But these were also among the most powerful in the country. And so, it was decided, the first step had to be to deal with them.

The lord Edward was dispatched to Stirling—this being a castle that could be taken only by blockade or by siege artillery. But Perth was a different case. The king's first attempt to take Perth had been very soon after his crowning, and it was his failure to do so that had ended with that disastrous defeat at Methven. It was only natural, therefore, that he should feel he was more than due his vengeance there!

I rode beside him as the march on Perth began—a long march, all the way from Inverness in the north to what was nearly the center of the country. It was rough going, too, for the men. But as always with the Bruce at their head, their spirits remained high. As did mine—until, that is, we actually arrived before the walls that enclosed both the castle and the city of Perth, and he ordered us to make camp there.

I stared in dismay at the prospect before us then. Those walls were around fourteen feet high. On one side of them flowed the River Tay—a river deep enough to take ocean vessels. On the other three sides was a moat as wide as the walls were high. That moat, too, would certainly also be deep! And so surely, I argued to myself, he was not going to repeat the mistake of that first attempt at Perth—the mistake of appearing before the city walls in force, yet still letting his army disperse sufficiently to be taken by surprise in the woods at nearby Methven.

We made camp, just as his first army had, and the guards patrolling the walls gathered to watch us doing so. And not only to watch! They cupped hands and shouted insults across to us, insults that grew all the more obscene as soon as they recognized that we had no siege machinery to batter the walls and so force them back into cover. And among their shouting I caught the words *"King Hob!"*

King Hob! That was the name for the fool they chose every May to be king of their frolics in the May Games! And that, too, was how their former king, old Edward I, had jeeringly christened Robert the Bruce when news of his becoming King of Scots had first reached England! I burned with shame and anger, and could not at all understand why the king should continue simply to keep us encamped there—day after day, too, with these taunts always continuing—and yet still seem so unconcerned over it all.

Nor, it seemed, could any of the others there, neither the officers nor the men. Yet what could any of us do except put our trust in him as much as we had always done? He had always before led us to victory, after all, as even the youngest and most recently joined of the army knew—in spite of which, I was still relieved when he ordered me off to find out and report back to him on the progress of the lord Edward at Stirling.

I rode south to Stirling, with its castle perched on the ridge of rock overlooking the town, and found the lord Edward's force well positioned to prevent supplies reaching it. Yet still, as I was told to report, its governor had given no sign of yielding to the blockade. My spirits sank even further at this, only to touch rock bottom when I arrived back at Perth to find our forces still encamped where I had left them. And still having to endure English taunts over "King Hob's army"!

To my surprise, however, the king simply smiled to see me now so downcast, and it was not till later that day that I understood the reason for this. Officers were assembled. The command was given for the army to march off, as if in retreat. But only *as if* in retreat, because that march would take it no farther than those Methven Woods of unhappy memory.

Once there, also, the men were to be told that this retreat was merely a feint to deceive the English into thinking we were now giving up in despair. But far from that being so, they were to start instead on making the scaling ladders needed for a surprise assault on the walls of Perth.

But what of the moat? The Douglas, Randolph, and Sir Robert Boyd all questioned him then. What of the wide and deep obstacle this was to any such assault? They would be told in good time the answer to that, the king assured them. And so the "retreat" began to an absolute torrent of jeers from the city walls, the English merchants who had settled in Perth joining happily in this with the soldiers there.

The short January day ran rapidly into the dark of a January night. It was cold in Methven Woods. The enclosing trees made darkness even deeper. Yet still, in spite of all this, the men obeyed the order against lighting fires. Quietly, instead, they hunched into their plaids till returning day would allow them to begin making the light scaling ladders the king had ordered.

I had just wrapped my own plaid around me when I became aware of an approaching figure. The king! He gripped my shoulder, and in a low voice he asked:

"Martin, do you remember a day when you stood alone with me against three men? Stood steady to obey the order I gave you then?"

Three men, all differently armed. And I, still only sixteen years old with no weapon except a bow and a few arrows! Yes, I told him, I did indeed remember. But remembering also that I had been frightened half to death that day, I added cautiously:

"And this time? What is it, Sire, that you want of me this time?"

"This time," he told me, "I need once more to have by me someone I can trust as I trusted you then. Someone I can rely on to make sure that the Douglas will avenge my death—if death *is* to be my portion. Because what I mean to do tonight is to wade that moat to test if there is any point where it is shallow enough for our whole army to wade it also."

Wade the moat! Wade that mud-bottomed ditch, stinking with rotten food thrown from every kitchen in Perth, the ordure of every latrine there, and God knows how many dead cats and dogs besides! Wade that cesspit of all cesspits. On his own, too, in the January cold and on a night as dark as the inside of a pocket! Yet what could I do to prevent him? He would not listen to anything I said on that score. And so what *could* I do except what he had asked of me?

Quietly together, we circled the camp. Quietly, the Bruce ordered an astonished guard post to let us pass towards the fields that eventually petered out into the rough moor that took us both, bent double, to the edge of the moat. Quickly, there, the Bruce stripped and stood naked except for the shirt he used then to tie around his loins. I passed him the belt that would help to hold this makeshift cover in place.

He bent to pick up the spear he had brought with him, then lowered himself into the moat—only to be immediately engulfed there. And he was well over six feet in height! I watched, in agony at my own helplessness to save him from drowning in that liquid mud. He surfaced and began striking out until, it seemed, his feet could touch bottom. And it was from there that he continued, with each step he took using his spear to test for depth in the one that followed.

I bundled up his discarded clothes and crawled alongside him, trying to keep track of his progress at the same time as I watched the bobbing lights from the lanterns carried by the guards patrolling the walls. A shout from one of these guards caused the king's form to disappear instantly under the moat's surface. In the same instant I fell flat under cover of my plaid, hoping that its dark color would make me also invisible.

The guard's shout was no more than an exchange of

pleasantries with another of his kind. And so it went on for what seemed to me an eternity of terror, with one alarm after another, but the king still determinedly wading and probing for almost two thirds of the moat's circumference. I was trying hard to keep a grip on the fear I had for him as well as for myself, when suddenly he paused at a point where the water reached only to his waist.

Some further steps he took then, probing all the time with his spear, but still the water was only waist high. I watched, in breath-held suspense while slowly he came towards me. He reached the moat's edge and began clambering onto the bank, gasping out as he did so:

"I was right. Habit—people are creatures of habit! And here is where they have been in the habit of tipping out enough waste to half fill the moat!"

He was mud covered from head to foot, and shivering so violently from cold that his teeth rattled on the words. "For God's sake, Sire!" I dropped his clothes to throw my plaid around him. I bundled the clothes again under one arm so that I could urge him with me back to the camp. And it was on our way there that I came to a decision.

"Sire, when you do make your planned assault, I want to be with you."

"Martin!" His mud-covered face jerked round in surprise towards me. "But you never take part in battle! Or not, at least, as a soldier."

"No more will I in this one, Sire. But if you can do what you did tonight, the very least *I* can do is to wade the moat again with you—and perhaps help a little by carrying the scaling ladder you will need then."

"Hmm," he said. And then, after a long moment, "If you feel you must, Martin. If you feel you must." After which we trudged on in what seemed to me to be a most companionable silence till we reached the camp and I had to hand him over to the care of Jean-Marie de Picard.

The assault was planned to take place at night, a week from that time—long enough to convince the castle garrison that our army really had departed, and that they could therefore relax their guard against us.

The men lined up with the scaling ladders they had made in the course of that week, all of them excitedly aware of the challenge the king had made to them as they worked. He would beat every man there, he had said, in the race to the top of these ladders! I shouldered the twelve-foot length of mine. A soldier hoisted up its other end. I saw Jean-Marie de Picard at the same task—for once, apparently, seized by the same spirit of competition that had all the others in its grip.

We moved off with the king in the lead, all of us treading as cautiously as he and I had the previous week, but heading this time for the part of the moat that he had proved could be waded. We had plastered mud on our faces so that these would not show up white against the pitch darkness all around us. And once the vanguard had reached the edge of the moat, the whole army kept strictly to the orders he had issued for crossing to its far side.

Those who carried the ladders went first, myself among them. The water came almost to my shoulders. I stumbled on the slime and unevenness of the rubbish underfoot—as did the man at the other end of the ladder. But still no sound escaped from either of us, and the other ladder carriers were equally silent.

On the far side of the moat we dispersed to place our ladders against the walls. I looked back from there and saw the rest of the army crossing in steady and orderly procession towards us. They dispersed as we had done, to regroup beside the ladders. I steadied the ladder that had the king's foot on its bottom rung and looked along the line of the walls.

The whole crossing had been accomplished in total silence and with almost unbelievable speed. Nor was there anything to be seen now of those who had made it except an impression of forms darkly merging with the darkness of the wall itself. The voices of guards sounded from above us. From there too, now, came the gleam of a swung lantern. And almost as if that had been like some sort of signal to him, the Bruce leapt upwards, sounding his war cry as he leapt.

I felt the ladder shake under his weight. I heard the repeated yells of that cry bursting out so loudly that my ears rang with the sound, and saw the dark mass at the foot of the wall break apart into a thousand dark shapes swarming upwards. From somewhere beyond the wall came the excited clangor of an alarm bell. From there, too, came shouts, screams, and the sound of wildly running footsteps.

A body came hurtling past me, the body of an English

soldier with a knife through his throat, and went splashing into the moat. I looked up to see flames bursting through the night's darkness. The castle on fire?

The attack, if that was so, was bound to be going now in favor of the Bruce—in which case he would not need the men he had left to hold the ladder heads against the possibility of having to retreat. I climbed to where these men remained perched on the city walls, and looked from there towards the castle.

The men of the garrison there had rushed out to escape the flames and were attempting some sort of rearguard action. Hopelessly, I realized, seeing also the tall figure of the Bruce at the forefront of the troops pressing against them. And besides, even if they did hold off his attack for a while, where did they have to run to?

I looked from the scene of battle to where the flames from the castle lit up the streets beyond, and saw the chaos that was there—people of all ages madly running, others stumbling about laden with household goods, yet still with the general trend of movement being towards the River Tay.

Where they might save their lives by trying to take ships back to England? Perth had been a town so wholly occupied by the English that this, I reckoned, was probably the impulse now among all these people. I watched grimly, my gaze going between the streets and the battle in front of the castle. The soldiers of the garrison began to lay down their arms. But it was only when the last of them had done so that the Bruce made his next move known.

From the beaten crowd before him then, he singled out the castle's governor and promptly had him hanged. But that, as he announced to all those looking up in awe to the dangling body, was only because the governor was a Scot and therefore a traitor to his lawful king.

As for all the English in the town, soldiers as well as others of the populace, they would have a choice. They could stay and suffer the same fate. Or they could depart instantly from Perth to make their way back as best they could to their own land.

"Never again to trouble me or my kingdom!"

It was with truly awesome contempt in his voice that he spoke these last words. And just as awesome was the sight of him towering there, all muddied from the moat, a raised sword still stained with the blood of victory giving point to all he said.

So there would be no more jeering talk of "King Hob." Not now. Not now that he had so spectacularly avenged the defeat of that first attempt to take Perth! I dropped down to the far side of the wall, wondering what further orders he might have for me, but it was not until many hours later that I was at last summoned to him.

"I owe you," he told me then. "I owe you for standing by while I waded that moat. And so I am going to give you even further responsibility."

"Sire!"

I bowed my acknowledgment of this, and with his voice continuing over the gesture, he told me, "I will need you more than ever now as swift rider between me and the Lord Chancellor in Arbroath. But the castles still to be taken stand widely separate from one another. I will therefore also need to keep contact with the commanders I mean to send against them. And that will be your responsibility—to form a band of messengers, and to train them in some of your own skills."

Ewen. The name leapt immediately to my mind. Ewen, who had proved at Barra Hill how hard he could ride—and who knew how to take charge of all the other gillies! I left the king with the determination to make him the first of my band of messengers, and went straightaway to look for him.

Chapter Fifteen

wen and I between us chose six of the brightest of our gillies. I left it to him to choose the fastest of the ponies for himself and those other six, then set about teaching them to move without the protection the army had always afforded them.

No direct approach to a castle, ways to avoid English patrols, the need to have a cover story always ready—these were some of the basic skills I drummed into them. I taught them also how to count, so that they could calculate time and distance. And finally the password they could give to anyone they judged they could trust—*"Brother Anselm sent me."*

I was kept equally busy, meanwhile, in riding back and forth on the comparatively short distance between headquarters in Perth and the Lord Chancellor in the small east-coast town of Arbroath. But with the king growing ever impatient to hear more about the lord Edward at Stirling, I was sent there also, at the end of March that year.

"Sire—" The news I had to deliver on my return was such

that I stumbled in my speech, and then brought it all out in one rushed statement. "The lord Edward has given up the blockade of Stirling Castle, his reason being a bargain he has made with its governor, Sir Philip Moubray. If, by midsummer of next year, no English force has appeared to relieve the castle, Moubray will surrender it without a blow struck."

"What?" Voice sharp as a whipcrack on the word, the king leant towards me. And then, as I began nervously to repeat my news, he exclaimed bitterly, "The fool! Oh, the fool!"

He was silent for a long moment, then, before he shot at me, "And his reason for such a bargain?"

The lord Edward, I had guessed, was quite simply bored with the tedious work of blockading. Added to which, as I had learned in Glen Trool, he was a romantic clinging still to the courtly and now-useless traditions in which he had been bred. But it was not my place, of course, to venture any such opinion to the king.

"As to that, Sire—" As woodenly as I could, I answered. "All I can say is what the lord Edward himself said I should tell you—that it was in order to free his forces for assault on the other castles still to be taken." There was another silence, then, before the king asked:

"You realize, do you, what this means?"

I nodded. The sack of Durham and all those other towns—that had been possible only because Edward of England had been at war with his barons. Yet it had still been a terrible blow to his pride, and now he no longer had that civil war on his hands. Now he had all the power he needed to challenge the contempt of him implied in this bargain.

"Yes, Sire," I said. "The English king will be a laughing-stock for everyone if he does not take advantage of your brother's bargain. And that means invasion."

"Exactly! And with Stirling as the supreme prize in that, I will be faced at last by the one situation I have striven for years to avoid—that of a pitched battle against superior forces. On ground, moreover, that is not of *my* choosing!"

"Unless—" Cautiously I put forward my own thought: "Unless, Sire, we first capture Stirling Castle ourselves."

"You are foolish, Martin. Even Longshanks himself could not take Stirling without heavy siege engines. And we have none of these. Nor can we waste further time in trying to starve out the garrison—not with all that still remains to be done before facing the massive force we can expect his son to bring against us."

I saw nothing of him after that for the full week that passed before the lord Edward came back from Stirling. I heard nothing, either, except for the angry shouting that went on behind closed doors then. But that was a week in which we all had time to realize the consequences of failing to defeat the English at Stirling.

They would continue not only to occupy the strongest castle in Scotland. The great force they would need to make sure of victory in that would spread out all over the land, and all our years of fighting would have been in vain.

I was all the more surprised, accordingly, to see how much the king's mood had changed by the time he called his next conference. Nor had he spoken there for long before it was clear that, far from continuing angry at being forced into pitched battle, he had come almost to welcome that prospect.

"Because," he declared in his opening speech to us, "I have fought for six long and hard years to win the amount of freedom we now have, yet with each battle always a gamble of skill against force. I have therefore thrown the dice in this for long enough. And if God has so willed that the battle we now face is the last throw I am to be allowed, I have faith enough in Him to bow gladly to that will."

They cheered him for that—all of them, in their admiration of his words, seemingly as prepared as he was to forgive the lord Edward *his* part in bringing about God's will. But, as he hastened then to warn them, the first step in preparing for that battle was to complete the work of capturing castles—because only then would he be able to summon the whole nation to arms. I looked to him for orders, and was told:

"The Chancellor will be able to gather much about the plans afoot in England, and so I need you still to ride swiftly between him and me. But if your messengers are now sufficiently reliable, your task is now also to use them in keeping touch with Randolph in Lothian, the Black Douglas in the border country, and the lord Edward at Dundee."

I began sending out my band, telling each one before he left, "Do not forget, either, that word of this coming invasion will spread, and so you must also keep both eyes and ears open for the effects of this on the people."

They were good lads, all of them. And gradually, as they

came back one by one with their reports, I was able to tell the king that even in Lothian, the most heavily occupied part of the land, the people were now doing more than speak of rebellion against their English overlords. They were actively aiding our forces there, and it was Ewen who came back with a report on the best example of all in this.

Binnock was the name of the man involved—William Binnock, the farmer who supplied hay to Linlithgow Castle. And it was through splutters of laughter that Ewen told me:

"So there is Binnock at the castle gate with his wagonload of hay, and a laddie—a wee boy of maybe ten or eleven—on the driving seat beside him. In the dawnlight as usual, with the porter on the gate still half asleep. "Open up there!" shouts Binnock, and the porter swings open the gate. Binnock drives forwards, but halfway through the gate, he stops the wagon. Down jumps the wee boy, an axe near as big as himself in his hand, and cuts the wagon's traces. The porter yells alarm and lets drop the portcullis. But the portcullis, of course, can fall only so far before it jams on that wagonload of hay!

"Then it's Binnock's turn to yell. *'Call all! Call all!'* he bellows, and out rush all the stout fellows he has planted in hiding around the castle. They swarm through the gate, scythes, spears, billhooks, axes—anything at all that can kill in their hands. And they make such short work of the garrison that the last seen of the ones that escaped, they were fleeing like frightened rabbits along the road to Edinburgh!"

The story ran right around the camp, ran with all the

speed and shock of summer lightning. I took the liberty of reporting it to the king in the very words that Ewen himself had used, and delightedly then he exclaimed:

"Now let us see if even Randolph or Douglas can match that for daring!" Because, of course, even though many of the castles in Lothian and the borders had already fallen to one or other of these heroes, the two that were most difficult of all to capture were still firmly in English hands.

There was Roxburgh, which dominated the whole border country. But Roxburgh was so openly situated that no attacking force could approach it unseen, and had walls so strong that these could be demolished only by heavy siege engines. There was Edinburgh, perched high on its rock above the town—a rock so sheer that no man, it was said, could climb it—and with its only entrance, the gate they called the East Port, so heavily garrisoned that it, too, required to be reduced by siege.

And meanwhile, as the date of invasion drew nearer, so did the news the Chancellor was gathering from England grow more and more ominous: . . . *an embargo to be put on the export of all English foodstuffs, wagons commandeered from twenty-one sheriffdoms, a muster of twenty-one thousand foot soldiers and four thousand archers, a further muster of two and a half thousand heavy cavalry* . . .

It was items like this in the dispatches I brought from the Chancellor's office that really made me fear for our situation now. Because, peacock vain as he was, this Edward of

England, and weak in strategy as his earlier invasions had also shown him to be, there was still no doubt that he was preparing now for battle on a truly massive scale. And how could a nation like ours possibly counter that?

Our population was only one tenth of England's. The core of our army had never consisted of more than around seven hundred men, with the Bruce always depending on adding to this when and wherever he could. But from all I had heard and seen of the information passing between king and Chancellor, we could not now hope to raise a force of more than seven thousand foot soldiers.

As for horse power! Fodder in our country was so scarce that the *destriers* I had helped to capture at Loudon Hill had long since been ransomed back to the English, and the most we could now raise of cavalry was some five hundred light horse.

"But give me a thousand men like Binnock," the king said cheerfully. "Give me, too, even five hundred like the lad with an axe 'near as big as himself,' and I will yet find *some* way to stop the English from coming to the relief of Stirling!"

I took heart again from this, remembering how often I had been witness to the fact that he never gave battle except in terms of a well-thought-out plan. And it was in this new mood of hope that I and my band rode with copies of the royal proclamation that mustered the whole nation to arms.

For weeks we rode, from south to north, from east to west, and took ship also to the chiefs of the clans in the islands of the northwest. In between journeys I reported to the king on the numbers to be expected from this or that part of the country, finding him sometimes at Perth, but more often at the site of the muster—near to Stirling Castle in the area they called "the Torwood." And with each time I reported there, the news that greeted me was good news—first in which was that the lord Edward had redeemed himself by capturing the castle at Dundee.

"The Douglas has taken Roxburgh Castle!" That, around the middle of March, was the next cry to greet me. But I knew Roxburgh. I knew it was impossible to approach this castle without being seen from its walls. And so how in the world had the Douglas force managed to reach it without being overcome by arrow fire?

"Easily!" It was my brother Sean who boasted thus, and this time with something really worth boasting about, since he had been one of the mere hundred men who had captured Roxburgh.

"The Douglas ordered all of our hundred to drape ourselves in black cloaks and crawl slowly, very slowly forward, over one of the fields around the castle. To make us look, he said, just like a herd of black cattle ambling home to the milking. And what with the time of day being dusk and a night mist beginning to rise from the River Teviot nearby, that was exactly what the guards on the walls took us to be!"

"But the walls themselves, those high walls," I objected. "You would have needed ladders to scale them. How could you carry scaling ladders under your cloaks?"

"Ask that of Sim of the Lead Howes!" Broadly grinning now, Sean brought out the name. "He was the lead miner that the Douglas found could make the ladders we used—rope ladders with wooden treads, and strong iron hooks fixed to the topmost tread. That topmost tread, too, carried an iron socket shaped like a spearhead. And so all we had to do was to crawl forward with the ladders rolled up under our cloaks. And then, with spearheads stuck into those sockets, we could raise them high enough to hook them onto the walls!"

"And once you were over the walls. Was there much of a fight?"

"Eh?" Sean glanced away from me for a moment, and then went blustering on, "Well, not for me. Not like some I've been in. The Douglas, you see, chose carnival as the time to attack—Shrove Tuesday, when the whole garrison was half drunk with the last of the wine they would have before Easter. And besides, our war cry was *'Douglas!'* And you know how the English always panic when they hear that!"

> *"Hush thee, hush thee, do not fret thee,*
> *the Black Douglas will not get thee. . . ."*

Had there, by any chance, been a soldier's wife thus singing lullaby to her child that night—singing somewhere quiet away from the din of carnival?

"There was!" Grinning still, when I spoke my thought aloud, Sean answered the question in it. "She was on the battlements, crouched down there nursing her baby when we scrambled over. And the next thing she knew was a mailed hand landing on her shoulder and the voice of the Douglas whispering, *'I would not be too sure of that!'*

201

I looked in horror at him. And quickly, defensively, he added, "But he was in jest, of course. And he left one of us there just to make sure no harm came to her."

There was something in his tone then—something that told me his real reason for saying that, for him, it had not been much of a fight.

"And *you* were the one," I guessed. "You protected that English soldier's wife."

"Aye," Drily he agreed. And then, in that same defensive tone, he added, "Well, English or not, she was still a woman, wasn't she? A woman with a bairn in her arms. And war or no war, what else could any decent man do?"

"Nothing else, Sean, nothing else," I told him. And throwing an arm around his shoulder, I walked beside him back to the campfire with the warm feeling that, at long last, he had learned to fight without hatred as his driving force.

It was the Douglas, of course, who was then the hero of the hour. Nor was there long to wait—two weeks only—before his friend and rival, Randolph, responded to that challenge.

"Edinburgh!" was the cry that went up then. *"Randolph has taken the castle of Edinburgh!"* And bit by bit, as his soldiers came marching back to camp, we learned the story behind that—the story of William Francis.

This Francis, it seemed, was a retired soldier who had once been a member of Edinburgh's garrison. And because he could not in those days get out of the castle to visit his lady love in town, he had found a way down the huge crag on which it was perched—the crag that everyone had said was unclimbable—then had followed that way up again.

"And when we heard about *that*," boasted the soldier who first told the tale, "we knew straightaway that we could do it too—if, that is, we could persuade Francis to lead us. Which wasn't hard to do, either, because he knew very well that we Highland lads can climb like cats."

And like cats they had indeed climbed, thirty of them following Randolph as the old soldier-turned-civilian showed them how to claw a way up to the battlements fringing that sheer and slippery face of black rock.

Only thirty? But ah, he assured us, Randolph had arranged for a diversion to take place—a supposed attack on the East Port. The moment the castle's soldiers rushed to combat this "attack," the thirty were over the battlements to take them in the rear—with the castle's governor the very first of the garrison to be killed. And, of course, in the confusion among the defenders then, it had been simple enough to open the East Port so that the bulk of Randolph's force could rush in to capture the castle.

The honors between the king's two heroes, it seemed, were now even! I watched the arrival of Randolph in camp— Lord Randolph, as he had become ever since the Bruce had made him Earl of Moray. I saw him and the Black Douglas throw their arms around each other before they went off together to greet the king. I heard the cheers that greeted this, but still could not help wondering then who were the real heroes of this year of the castles.

Most certainly, I decided, that must include the king himself. But what about ordinary fellows like that farmer William Binnock? What about Sim of the Lead Howes, with his clever design of those scaling ladders? And what about William Francis, no longer young but still daring to put courage to the test by leading that climb?

I found my gaze wandering over the thousands of men now gathered in the Torwood—men who would soon be called on to prove themselves as heroic as these three. Yet most of them had no previous experience of soldiering, could not even visualize an English cavalry charge—the wave upon wave of mounted men hurling at them what would literally be tons of steel. How could the king even think of leading them into a battle where they would be so vastly outnumbered?

I had the answer to my question in one word, a word I heard roared out again and again as he daily addressed these same men.

"Drill! You will drill, and drill, and drill again in the tactics I plan to use against the English army. You will drill until you drop to the ground. But at least when you do drop, you will still be alive. As you will be alive also on that very ground, God willing, when He grants us our victory there!"

Chapter Sixteen

We were ready for them long before they came on that Midsummer's Day in the year of Our Lord thirteen hundred and fourteen—all of our four companies placed to guard the road to Stirling Castle.

The Bruce's own company was at the southern end of the New Park—the highest part of the wooded land rising gently for the mile lying south and west of the castle. North of him from this point—the Borestone, as they called it—were our other three companies, with the lord Edward, the Black Douglas, and Randolph as their commanders.

Facing the New Park, and stretching for well over a mile to the south and east of the castle, was the Carse of Stirling— ground that was much too boggy for any army to be marched across it. Rising from the Carse to make a plateau of firm ground was the broad plain that carried the road to the castle, and that would be ideal for English cavalry. But to reach that plain, the English would first have to ford the stream known as the Bannock Burn, and there were only two places where cavalry riding in formation could do so.

One was where it ran across the road beyond the southern extremity of the New Park, and was thus overlooked by the king's position. The other was at the far end of the deep and rocky gorge that then carried its winding course past the village of Bannock and so into the Carse. But for the English to reach that other ford would mean having first to march through woodland—a most difficult maneuver for an army of the size *they* had. And it was on all these factors that the king had based his plan to stop them reaching the castle.

His own company, he had decided, would try to hold them at the ford overlooked from the Borestone. If they passed him there, the lord Edward and the Douglas would attack their flank, and if the flank attack failed, Randolph would stand face to face with them on that road to the castle.

There was one other approach to the castle, however, that might just have figured in whatever plans the English had. That was the bridle track winding along between the Carse and the plain and almost concealed from view by the way the ground of the plain rose above it. But again, as the king had pointed out, there was no army in full battle order could be marched along so narrow a way.

"And yet," thoughtfully, afterwards, he had added to this, "if they try—as might well be the case—to send a picked cavalry force along it, and if that force reaches the castle, they could then claim to have relieved it according to the bargain made with its governor. And so, Randolph, since your position is the one nearest that track, you must place scouts to guard it."

That had been at dawn, when we had first mustered. Now it was well into afternoon, with the fierce sun of that June day creating a shimmer of heat haze all around the towers and turrets of the castle. The English, our scouts had earlier reported, were only fifteen miles off, and a later reconnaissance by the Douglas had verified the size of their army.

So huge was this, he had reported then, that even their wagon train stretched out for twenty miles. But that had been two hours ago. And slow as *must* be the pace of so enormous a force, that meant they must surely be very near us now. I was sweating, I realized, and not just from the great heat of the day! With a hand raised to wipe my brow, I recalled what the king had said when the Douglas had reported to him.

"Keep this from the men!" Low-voiced and hurried that instruction had come. And so what had his thoughts been then? What were they now that the English were almost on us with more than three times the number of footmen we had, and five times the amount of heavy cavalry against our five hundred of light horse? Did he still think there was a chance—any chance at all—of preventing them from reaching that castle?

I stared towards where he had positioned himself at the outermost edge of the Borestone. He had left his battle-horse—the charger procured for him by his Marischal, Sir Robert Keith—in the shade of the woods behind us, and his mount then was only the gray pony he used for riding in review of his troops. But even so, there was still no mistaking the grandeur of his presence.

He was armored, with the heraldic beast of Scotland—the lion rampant—blazing red against the white of the surcoat over his armor. The crown that proclaimed him King of Scots circled his helmet in a glittering band of gold. He sat so tall in the saddle, too, even on that small mount. And yet, it was still none of all this that suddenly brought back to me all the confidence I had always felt in him.

He had been wise, I had realized, not to have disheartened the men by letting them know how fearful were the odds against them—wise enough simply to trust as much to their courage as they had always trusted his leadership. And as they trusted also, of course, to that sixth sense he had so often shown—that sense of seeming always to know just how and when to strike at the enemy!

He was sitting very still—so still, indeed, that he might have been the statue of a man on a horse—except, that is, for the slow movement of his head, always turning this way and that as he kept constant survey of the terrain below him.

From my position just behind him, I saw his gaze fix at one point of the far side of that plain of firm ground rising above the Carse—one point where the edge of the plateau made by this rise might just have allowed for a glimpse of the bridle path beyond it. And then, suddenly, so suddenly that I almost jumped out of my skin, the statue came to life.

"Cavalry!" His voice roaring, one arm outflung, he pointed across the plateau and towards the bridle path. I rode forward but saw nothing. Yet still he was insisting, "Cavalry on the bridle path—there, where I saw the flutter of their pennons as they passed." Furiously, he swung towards me to order, "Warn Randolph! Warn him to bar their way!"

I wheeled my black, Snapper, and struck spurs to him. The king's voice, as the creature bounded off, came after me.

"Be swift to report back. And tell Randolph from me that a rose has fallen from his chaplet!"

And how true *that* was! Randolph, the rose-crowned hero of so many victories, had obviously failed now in that simple task of setting scouts to guard the bridle path. Randolph was allowing English cavalry to reach Stirling Castle, and thus— as the king had warned—to be able to claim that it had been relieved!

I reached Randolph's company still without having glimpsed that cavalry for myself, the plateau for most of its length continuing too high above the bridle path to allow for any sight of it. But even so, I had no need to shout my message to him—perhaps because the speed of my approach had combined with his own feelings of guilt to warn him into action.

Already he was mounted and leading a company of spear- men in a race towards the bridle path. I followed in their tracks and watched their instant assembly there into two close-packed ranks of men, the front rank kneeling with the butts of their spears dug into the ground and the spears them- selves held at just the level for plunging into the belly of a charging horse. The second rank stood close behind the first, their spears outthrust over the heads of the kneeling men, the points of those spears directed to what would be chest level for a mounted man.

It was the *schiltrom* formation taught to them by the Bruce—a formation that could be altered instantly to that of either a hollow square or hollow circle, all according to the signals given by an easily visible mounted commander. And which thus, of course, from whatever angle it was tackled, would be equally deadly.

Behind this formation, also, Randolph had placed a body of archers. I heard him order these to stand ready to fire, and in that same moment I saw the English cavalry.

They were coming on at quite a leisurely pace—trusting, perhaps, to whatever locally gained knowledge had told them they could ride there undetected from wherever our army might be. And just as the Bruce had forecast, they were indeed a picked force.

The figured metal of their armor glittered in the sun. Gold shone from the plating of their spurs. The pennants they flew gleamed in bright heraldic colors, as did the saddlecloths draped over the flanks of their horses. Altogether, indeed, and sitting high as they did on these huge *destriers*, they looked like a company of gods. And couched under each right arm was a lance, swinging from each saddle bow was a mace—a huge and solid ball of spiked steel!

At the sight of the *schiltrom* blocking their way, however, their pace slowed even further, until finally it came to a halt. They sat, then, near enough for me to see even the faces beneath the pushed-back visors of their helmets—faces that now wore an expression of astonished arrogance. As if, I thought, they simply could not believe that mere men—and simple spearmen at that—should dare even to think of challenging all that might, all that display of military splendor. And then just as that thought went through my mind, they pulled down the visors of their helmets, closed ranks, and charged.

I heard the voice of Randolph roaring, *"Stand firm! STAND FIRM FOR BRUCE AND SCOTLAND!"*

And the *schiltrom* stood firm!

Shoulder pressed to shoulder, as the Bruce had taught them in all those weeks of drilling till they dropped, they remained with each spear in that thick hedge of spears held steady as rock against the wave of horseflesh and steel surging towards them. With a sound that could have been imagined only in a nightmare—a mingling of men's voices yelling, horses screaming, and the crashing sound of metal against metal—the charge impacted against those massed spearpoints. Yet still that mass did not break.

It was the charge that broke, instead, to the noise of yet more clanging of metal, yet more frantic screaming as horses were impaled and their riders sent hurtling to the ground. From the rear of the *schiltrom*, also, came flights of arrows directed at the cavalry's rear ranks. And fired at that short range, these arrows sent yet more of the riders toppling.

There were some five hundred, however, in that cavalry force, more than sufficient for them to regroup and charge again—and again, and yet again. But not, finally, on the narrow front imposed on them by the confines of the bridle path. This time they were going to try instead to surround the *schiltrom* and attack it from any angle they could.

From behind me, as they prepared for this, I heard shouts and the thud of feet running. I turned, to see the Douglas racing towards me at the head of a force from his own company. Coming to the aid of his friend, Randolph, I realized, and turned again to see how much that aid might eventually be needed.

Randolph, at the first sign of that different form of attack, had re-formed his *schiltrom* into a hollow circle, with himself and his archers at its center. The cavalry men came thundering towards this circle spreading out as they did so in an attempt to break it from as many points as possible.

But the ground to their right was the squelching bog of the Carse, and horses cannot charge over bog. The ground to their left was the peaty slope leading up to the plain, and the crumbling surface of peat dried by summer suns gives no footing to anything as heavy as a *destrier*. And still, with horsemen slipping and stumbling all around then, still with Randolph directing arrow fire at the nearest of them and only the occasional closing up of ranks needed to compensate for a fallen spearman, the *schiltrom* stood firm.

The Douglas brought his mount to a sliding halt beside me. And gaspingly then, as his men began to catch up with him, he demanded:

"How goes it with Randolph?"

"As you see, sir." I pointed down to where those splendid

knights on horseback around the *schiltrom* had been reduced by then to the desperate hope that at least some of its men would be killed by the maces and even swords they were now hurling into its midst. The Douglas looked from there to where mailed bodies and brightly caparisoned horses lay strewn everywhere around the scene of battle. And then, with that lean, dark face of his breaking into a smile, he said cheerfully:

"It took time for me to get the king's permission to come to his help. But now, it seems, there is no need at all for that!"

From my brother, Sean, the first of those to form up behind him, came a loud groan of disappointment. From those behind Sean came echoes of this feeling, until the Douglas shamed it into silence by calling out:

"You are spoiling for action, I know. But the lord Randolph has already won the day, and so it is he alone who should now be able to claim the victory."

But did the English know that the Douglas was too chivalrous to seize on the chance of even a share in what was due to his friend? Evidently not, I realized—not from the way that, with many a backward glance at the Douglas reinforcements, some of them were already riding off!

The first desertion of the scene was quickly followed by more, and yet more, until the last of the cavalry force was in full retreat. And then, madly eager to go in pursuit, the *schiltrom* did break. It was against all the rules of war, after all, for infantry to defeat cavalry. Quite unheard of, indeed— for those, that is, who did not know of Loudon Hill!

So I thought, at least, watching Randolph restrain his men

from the impossible task of pursuing the fleeing cavalry. And then, remembering the further duty that had been laid on me, I left them all busily wiping off sweat and congratulating one another while I rode back to the Borestone to make my report to the king.

He nodded acceptance, sitting there on his gray pony in front of the company he had in readiness to repel any further force of cavalry advancing by way of the ford. And indeed, there was already some sign of that—a murmur of sound that carried well in the still air of that hot afternoon. The king sat for a further few moments, head inclined as if better to identify the sound. And then, to Sir Robert Boyd beside him, he said briskly:

"Take command, Boyd, while I make reconnaissance."

"Sire!" In wild alarm as the king urged his pony forwards, Sir Robert made a futile grab at its bridle rein. But as if this gesture of protest had not even registered with him, the king continued down the long and gentle slope of grass leading to the ford. Sir Robert swore, and said bitterly:

"As if he could not have sent scouts to do that!"

I made no immediate answer to this. I watched for several moments in silence instead as the figure on the gray pony rode on, and then could not forbear to say:

"You were at Perth, Sir Robert. And it was not a scout who probed for us the depth of the moat there."

"But listen—listen now! And look there!"

I listened, and distinctly heard the sound of jingling metal. I looked to where he was pointing—the rise of ground that led down to the south side of the ford. I saw banners flying. And then, topping that rise, I saw the reason for that—an English cavalry force in their advance towards the ford. And our king was now nearer to them than he was to us!

With one hand raised high, the leader of that metaled horde brought its advance to a halt. He had seen the figure on the gray pony. He glanced up towards the Borestone, his head in its great, crested helmet tilted towards our position there.

"I know him!" Boyd gasped. "I know him by that crest on his helmet—Sir Henry de Bohun, nephew of the Earl of Hereford."

The glance of the knight de Bohun went back to the gray pony and its rider—the rider whose helmet carried not a crest, but a golden crown. In a swift movement then, de Bohun couched his lance under his right arm.

Boyd gasped again. "The crown! He has recognized the king by his crown. And he is going to charge!"

But surely the king, too, had realized that. And so why did he not turn and ride as hard as he could to his own ranks? De Bohun was mounted on a *destrier*. The king rode only a pony. Both men were fully armored, but de Bohun had a lance, a mace, a sword, while the king's only weapon then was a light axe.

"And so why does he *not* ride to safety!"

I spoke aloud, without realizing I was doing so. And with a groan now in his voice, Boyd answered, "Because he can see that de Bohun's idea is to settle the whole affair by challenge to single combat. Because the Bruce will not stain his honor by refusing that challenge."

The *destrier* had moved forwards and was quickening its pace. The gray pony was also moving—but moving towards it, and so drawing from Boyd an even louder gasp of dismay. At the same time, also, from among all those who had come crowding around us, came the anguished voice of Sir Walter of Ross.

"I cannot watch! I cannot bear to watch further!" I saw him drop his face into his hands, and wanted to do the same. Yet still, in a sort of fascinated horror at the very fact of so unequal a contest, I could not help continuing to stare at the scene below.

The pace of both the *destrier* and the pony had quickened into a gallop. De Bohun, with his lance held rigidly advanced, was tensed for the moment when, according to all the rules of a joust between knights, the two would pass right flank to right flank and that lance would be sent thrusting through the king.

But one thing that de Bohun did not know—or else had forgotten—was that, for the past eight years and under all sorts of conditions, his opponent had practically lived in the saddle. And that opponent was not now fighting in any knightly joust. He was King Robert the Bruce, fighting for his life, his throne, his country!

With the point of the lance so close that there would be only seconds before it pierced him, the Bruce swerved his mount to make it pass on the *destrier*'s left. And rising to his full height in the stirrups as it did so, he brought the axe in his left hand crashing down on de Bohun's helmet.

Such was the force of that blow, also, that the axe blade sliced right through the metal of the helmet to split de Bohun's head in two. The shattered corpse swayed drunkenly, then toppled. The *destrier* floundered on, dragging it by the mailed foot still stuck in one of its stirrups. The Bruce, with no more than a glance for what he had done, rode swiftly back to the Borestone.

"I am sorry my good axe is broken." Calmly, then, holding the splintered axe shaft up to view, he shrugged off both the cheers for his feat and the reproaches for the terrible risks it had entailed. "But see there!" The axe shaft swung round to point at the cavalry still in position beyond the ford. "See how they now still hesitate to advance!"

And indeed, that cavalry force *was* still hanging back— dismayed, no doubt, by the terrible death of their leader. We could see also now that their numbers were large. Abruptly then, the king turned to rap out an order to me. The lord Edward's company was immediately to reinforce his own, the Douglas was to stand ready for his being the sole one to make the flank attack.

I wheeled my mount in obedience to the command. And looking back over my shoulder as I rode, I had my last glimpse of what was happening then—our whole company racing down to give battle against the English cavalry, with the golden crown of the king bobbing in the lead of their advance.

Chapter Seventeen

The order delivered to the lord Edward and the Douglas, I waited where I knew the king would make his last stand—if, that is, the English cavalry broke through and if he was still alive by then. I stood beside Randolph, with both of us having to rely then on various of my messenger band for news of the fierce and bloody mêlée raging at the ford.

A long wait we had of it, too, before word came that the English cavalry had finally been repelled and that the king had called his officers to meet him at the Borestone. I rode back there with Randolph, to hear the king plunging immediately into plans for the following day.

Our scouts, he reminded us, had reported that the English now had two days of forced marches behind them. Now also, it was too late in the day for them to get all their great army into position for a battle that could well last for hours. Nor could they fight any such battle without first finding water for both men and beasts.

Further, he pointed out, the only available water was that of the Bannock Burn, and except for the two points at which this could be forded, its banks were too high to allow animals down to drink from it. All of which, since they had failed to pass us at the ford below the Borestone, had left them with no alternative now except that of making camp by the ford at the far side of the gorge.

"And from there," he finished, "to try tomorrow to gain that plain of firm ground so perfect for their cavalry."

There were nods of agreement then, from everyone present there. And boldly then also, the lord Edward pointed out, "But the spirits in that camp tonight will not be of the highest. Not on the soggy ground it offers—and especially not when the men learn of the shame we have already put on their cavalry!"

"Agreed, brother. But consider also"—a new note had entered the king's voice, a note of warning—"that cavalry was only their advance force. And once they do gain that plain, they can send the whole might of it against us."

He paused there, to let his gaze rest on each man in turn. He was smeared with peat mud, his hair and beard matted with sweat—just as he had been on the day I rescued him from the peat hag. And the faces he surveyed now were those who had shared in all he had suffered and fought for since then—old comrades in arms like Boyd, Randolph, and the Douglas, newer recruits like Sir Walter of Ross, the Moray men he had led to victory at Barra Hill, the Highland chiefs who had rallied their men to fight for him after his victory over John of Lorn.

"Some of you here now," he said quietly, "are those who fought and bled with Wallace. All of you I have led, at one time or another, into battle. Those two victories we have gained today, also, would now allow us to retreat with honor from the enormous host assembled against us. And I, for one, would not blame any man who chose to do so."

He paused again, as if to lend even greater weight to his words, and then finished, "What I want you to tell me now, therefore, is this. Do *you* wish to retreat with honor—but so also to lose everything we have gained over the past seven years? Do *you* wish to start the struggle all over again—and if we are finally defeated in that to live the rest of your lives as slaves? Or do you wish to fight tomorrow—and if you die then, to die as free men?"

"To fight! To fight! To fight!" With one voice, in a mighty surge of sound, they answered him. And barely had that sound died away before he announced:

"In that case, I will no longer conceal from the men the true size of the force against them. Because each of these, too, has the right now to make his own decision."

Off he strode then, to make the same speech to the men as he had to the officers. He went to ask them too, if they would rather live as slaves or die as free men. And got from each company in turn the same response as from his officers.

So loud did they roar that response, too, that the English at the ford on the far side of the gorge might well have taken the echo of it as a signal for an attack on their camp there. Or so our scouts later reported, at least, because none of their army that night had disarmed, nor even unbitted their horses. Nor had they slept—although, the ground there being so boggy, sleep in any case would have been impossible for them.

But neither, of course, did our army sleep that night, all of it being so tense in anticipation of carrying out the king's battle plan for the next day. Besides which, after the men had all been fed and watered, the hours of summer darkness were too few to be used for anything apart from schooling them in all the details of that plan.

I listened to the king expounding it first to his officers and marveled at the audacity of it. To desert the position that gave him the cover of the woodland, and instead of defending himself against the English to launch an attack on them—surely only he could have conceived of anything so bold. And surely only he had the eye for the terrain on which he had based that plan!

But what of myself in all this? I could not, would not, play the part of soldier. But even so, the coming battle would be so utterly, so finally decisive that there must surely be *something* I could do in it?

"And keep this also in mind," the king finished. "The enemy does not yet know how small our force is compared to theirs. And so, when your companies march out to the attack, I want each of them to make a brave show of banners."

A brave show of banners! A memory of Brother Anselm flashed into my mind—riding with the old man to Ayr, and him telling me then that the size of an army was judged by the number of banners it brought to the field. And did we not have, in the rear of our army, another great company that could also make a brave show of banners?

"Sire—" With the officers dismissed, I began trying to put to the king the idea that had leapt into my mind—but only to find he had already thought of this.

"Yes, Martin," he told me, "but they are not organized and drilled troops of the line. Nor can I spare even one officer now to bring them into order—and also to judge the moment when they will be of most use to me. But you . . ." He paused, his eyes keenly on me. "Even though you will not fight," he finished, "you have all the qualities needed in a leader of men. And so it is to you, now, that I *must* entrust that task."

My heart singing over his words, I raced Snapper the short distance to the hollow between the two highest points of the New Park—Gillies Hill and Coxet Hill. And there they were, mingling with our gillies and camp orderlies, the great company of "small folk," too poor to arm themselves properly as soldiers, but who had yet rallied eagerly to fight in any way they could for the Bruce. They knew me, too—knew from my messenger band that I was the king's swift rider, trusted implicitly to convey his commands.

I plunged forwards, calling them all around me, and began showing them how, with blankets and even shirts tied onto long pieces of stick, they too could make a brave show of banners!

Dawn, the first hint of dawn, saw the army assembled to hear Mass. The priest with the king's company was the chaplain of his own household. Like all the other priests there, he wore armor under his robes. His voice, as he began reading from Isaiah the lesson for that day, trembled on the words "Comfort ye, comfort ye my people. . . ." The king, at the end of the service, spoke briefly and soberly to us all.

"I have sent to all my commanders," he said, "to tell them to speak to their men as I speak to you now. Our country can raise no more fighting men than are mustered here today. Against us we have the greatest army that England could raise, or ever will be able to do so again. Defeat for us today will therefore mean the end of Scotland. I beg you, therefore, to pray to God before you fight. Face manfully to the enemy. And with His help and the help of all our Scottish saints, we will yet gain the victory that will make us once again a free nation."

We ate in silence the rations that were issued then. Jean-Marie de Picard led out the king's war charger. Sir Robert Keith, the Marischal, departed for the position assigned to our five hundred of horse. The Royal Standard was raised. And three of our companies, in response to this signal, went marching out of the woods.

I stayed at the Borestone, where the king was holding his own company in reserve, knowing that only from there could I observe events and thus be able to judge my own time for action.

The three companies' formation was that of an inverted wedge, all of it intended to force the English back from the broadest part of the plain and into the loop of ground that had the gorge on its right and rising terrain on its left. Randolph rode at the head of the company forming the left side of the wedge. The company forming its right side was led by the lord Edward.

The company headed by the Douglas formed the center of the wedge. It marched slightly behind as well as between the other two, so that he could observe and judge just when it would be needed to help in repelling the English cavalry. Above all three companies, as the king had commanded, flew the bright colors of many banners.

From the English camp, as this army emerged from the wood, came the loud call of an alarm trumpet. The three companies reached the edge of the plain. The commanders signaled a halt, then slid from their horses to join every other man there in dropping to their knees. From among the kneeling men, one strong voice called out the opening words of the Lord's Prayer—the only one that all these men had in common.

"*Pater noster, Qui es in coelis* . . . Our Father which art in heaven . . ." At the great murmuring surge of voices joining that first one, all of us at the Borestone—the king included—also knelt, and began praying along with them. " . . . *et dimitte nobis debita nostra . . . sed libera nos a malo . . .* Forgive us our trespasses . . . but deliver us from evil . . ."

As the prayer continued to its end, the alarm calls from the English camp grew both in number and volume. Our forces remained kneeling till the prayer was finished, as did the king also. And it was only when the Amen had been spoken that he rose to mount his war charger.

"There he is—Edward of England himself!" He pointed to the English king's standard flying above a group of horsemen stationed at the point where the ground on the far side of the gorge rose highest.

"And there—" The pointing hand stabbed down towards our three companies, once more on their march into battle. "There is the very last thing he must have expected to see—our little army daring an open attack on *his* great force!"

Our three companies were surging forwards now over the half mile of plain that formed the widest part of the battle-front. At the far side of the plain, where it sloped sharply down to the soft ground of the Carse and the ford over the Bannock Burn, came the first appearance of the English cavalry. But just as the king had reckoned, of course, the haste needed to counter the surprise of our dawn attack had caused such confusion that this cavalry was no more, as yet, than a disorderly mass.

Randolph and the lord Edward, nevertheless, had immediately re-formed their men into *schiltroms*. Like this, they continued their forward march. And it was even as they did so that various points in the whole scene burst simultaneously into action.

Confusion there may have been in the English camp. But somebody, at least, must have got their archers into place. And somebody, too, was now managing to bring the cavalry into the order needed for their first charge. From where the archers must have camped overnight—the wooded ground on the lord Edward's right—the advancing *schiltroms* were attacked by flight after flight of arrows. And from the far side of the plain came the trumpet call that sounded the charge.

The *schiltroms* wavered under the archers' attack, but did not break. The cavalry began its charge. From the woods below, where the king had anticipated the presence of the archers, came the horn call that signaled our five hundred horse to attack them.

The cavalry charge gathered speed. The *schiltroms* halted to meet the charge. The aim of the English archers, under the assault of our horsemen, grew ever wilder, with some arrows now striking among their own cavalry. The charge thundered on, regardless, its right wing aiming for the Scottish left under Randolph, its left wing aiming for the Scottish right under the lord Edward.

The air cleared altogether of arrows. The lord Edward's *schiltrom* took the first shock of the charge. Seconds later, like some giant wave meeting rock, the English right wing broke on Randolph's *schiltrom*. And into the space between the two came that of the Douglas, closing up the line of advance and pushing this mercilessly forward.

I stared out over the plain beyond it to the mass of cavalry now milling around there. And even though I had heard the night before every detail of the king's plan, it was only then that I realized the true brilliance of its concept.

To the confusion caused by the surprise of our attack there was now being added a further confusion. The cavalry still at the foot of the slope leading from their camp to the plain could not see what was happening among those already there.

Yet still they were pushing their horses up that slope—thus cramping still further those who had been forced to withdraw and try to re-form for another charge against the *schiltroms*. And cavalry, to be effective, *had* to have room to maneuver.

From the higher terrain on the English right, also, our own archers were now pouring down rapid fire on these attempts. And with every step our advancing *schiltroms* took, they were increasing their chances of pinning the enemy into the loop of ground that had the higher terrain on one side and the gorge on the other. But could they really succeed in doing so?

That horde of cavalry had brave men among it—many of them—brave men who were also experienced soldiers. And I could see now that, even lacking the overall direction that would have pulled them together for a massed charge, they had still managed to form the groups that were thundering again into attack. It was the Scottish right, too, that was now most threatened—the lord Edward's force. And if that broke . . .

The king, his sword drawn and pointing the way, roared out, "The English left! Forward to attack on the English left!"

I stayed still as stone to let the whole of his company stream past me. With one thought only in my mind, I watched them clash with the English left. This was our reserve force. And for the king thus to commit his reserve *must* mean that he had judged the battle as beginning to turn against those already engaged. I wheeled Snapper and raced him to where I would find my company of "small folk."

Ewen and my other messengers had obeyed my instruction to have them all lined up ready for me. Each of them had a weapon of some kind—an axe, a scythe, a billhook—work tools, in fact, now to be put to deadlier use. Every other one of them was hefting a makeshift banner. Ewen thrust one into my hand—a sturdy pole with a piece of bright-red blanket tied to it. I raised this high, and shouted:

"Remember what I said. You must make the English think you are yet another company of trained troops coming to the attack. And so march now as soldiers do. Do not run. MARCH!"

They marched, myself leading, using both hands to hold my banner aloft and guiding Snapper with my knees. The scene below, as we came out of the woods, was a nightmare vision of men and horses all crammed into the loop of ground between the gorge and the plain's higher terrain, horses rearing, weapons waving, and rising from all this a din of battle so loud that it seemed almost to burst my eardrums.

My company kept formation. We reached the edge of the conflict. From somewhere in the midst of it I saw suddenly a flash of gold. And from where that gold flashed came the voice of the Bruce roaring:

"On them! On them! They fail! They fail!"

There was no way then, I knew, of restraining my company. There were Highlanders among them, and no one can keep a Highlander out of a fight! They rushed on, yelling, their crude weapons held high. Snapper was swept along with them. In panic, he reverted to his old savage habit of biting. I pulled his head up, wrenching one-handed at the reins and trying with the other hand to keep my flag aloft. Snapper reared, throwing me violently from the saddle. My head struck hard on the ground. I had a fleeting sensation of sleepiness, and then—nothing.

I do not know how long I lay senseless there, nor indeed how long it took me to recover from the stupor that held me afterwards. All I was aware of, in fact, was the sounds of battle still continuing and then dying away to the point where I knew I must force myself to try and discover its outcome.

I rose and began a stumbling way over blood-stained grass littered all over with corpses of men and horses. But among this horrible detritus of battle there were also the clearest of all signs of victory for our side—the groups of English knights sitting disconsolate under guard of our own men. And it was from these guards that I learned of what I had missed in the progress towards that victory.

The Bruce? Thank God, they answered my first query, he was alive and unwounded—as indeed were all his commanders. And what had happened after my company came marching out of the woods?

I listened then, as well as my dazed condition would allow, while they went on to tell that this was the very point when it seemed that the battle could have gone either way. But then, just as the king had hoped would happen, the English had wavered at the sight of what seemed to be yet another reserve being thrown at them. And it was the final onslaught the king had called for then that had broken them.

It was the sheer size of their force, moreover, that had turned their attempted retreat then into a rout. Because, trapped as they were in that loop of ground, there was no way that the mass of them could back from the merciless pressure of the *schiltroms*. And with nothing except the gorge on their left flank, it had not been possible, either, for hundreds of them to escape being hurtled down to their deaths there.

As for their enormous army of foot soldiers, all of these—without attempting to strike even a single blow—had also fled. Because what could foot do against a force that had already put its cavalry to flight—especially when the English king himself had joined in that flight?

"But not willingly!" With a sort of grudging admiration, one of our men added this to his part in the tale. "He is a fool, that man, but no coward, because—I saw it for myself—it took two of his knights to drag him off the field of battle."

"And our king," I asked, "where is he now?" The soldier pointed to Stirling Castle. "There—taking the surrender from its governor."

So now it was all over! Scotland, at last, was free. And so now I, too, was free—free of putting duty first, free to start the quiet life of study I would have led if I had not long ago been moved by the plight of a hunted man—and if that man had not turned out to be Robert the Bruce, King of Scots!

Seven years I had spent with him since then, seven hard and dangerous years. But in those years also I had grown more and more to admire him, and to share in his passion for freedom—even to love him as I might have loved the father I had never really had the chance to know. And so it had been worthwhile, had it not, to give all that time of service to him—much, much more worthwhile than the boy who first went with him could ever have dreamed would be the case. Yet even so, it was time now to take my last leave of him.

I called Snapper to me, meaning to ride there and then to the castle. One of the guards, as I mounted, asked curiously:

"You're Martin, are you not? Martin Crawford—brother to our officer, Sean Crawford?"

Sean—I had forgotten about him! I turned swiftly to ask if he was still alive, and got an immediate chorus of reassurance on this.

"In that case"—I kicked heels to Snapper—"tell him good-bye from me!"

"A minute, Martin!" A shout from one of them arrested my move. "The soldier who rode at the head of the 'small folk'— the one with the big red banner. Your brother has been asking about him—wondering if *he's* still alive."

"The one with the banner?" I hedged for a moment, thinking of what to say. And then, urging Snapper on again, I called back, "Oh, him! Yes, he's still alive. But he was no soldier—just some young fellow who had agreed to give the king whatever help he could."

The guard's voice shouted after me, "He was brave all the same, your brother says, and would have made as good a soldier as any of us."

I waved to show I had heard him. And then, as swiftly as I had ever done, I rode on to Stirling Castle and the release to my new life that all my knowledge of the Bruce told me would willingly be granted there.

Epilogue

Epilogue

I t was towards the end of my ninth year as Abbot of Melrose Abbey that I was told of a company of soldiers arriving there and of their officer demanding to see me. He was shown into my study. And even though I had been half expecting some such visit, I was still taken aback to see that this officer was my brother, Sean.

We eyed each other over the width of my study desk, each of us taking in the changes over the sixteen years since we had last met. He spoke first, defensively telling me:

"I do not know what to call you. 'My lord Abbot'? 'Father Martin'? Which is correct?"

I waved him to a chair and answered, " 'Martin' will do. Or, if you prefer it, I would not mind hearing you say 'little brother.' "

He smiled at that, and glanced around my study— bare of any other furnishings apart from an illuminated text on one wall. "I had not thought," he said, "that a lord

Abbot would live so sparely."

"Some do," I told him. "Some do not."

He enquired then about Shona, but my news there was no different from what his occasional visits to her had already told him. Shona, as I had hoped, had indeed become a different person since the king's victory at Bannockburn—as we had now become accustomed to name that battle—had won the release of the Princess Marjorie. Shona had long since come out of the protective shell of childhood. But even so, as the Prioress of her convent had continued to write to me, she was still content to stay there, and they were still glad to have her.

But it was not to enquire about Shona, of course, that he had come. And with a loud clearing of his throat when I had finished speaking about her, he rose and placed on my desk a small silver box.

"I have brought this," he said, "all the way from Granada in Spain. And now I have been sent by Lord Randolph, Earl of Moray, to deliver it to you. Because this Abbey of Melrose is the one that the Bruce always loved best, and you are its Abbot. And so you, the Lord Randolph has informed me, will know what to do with it."

I sat staring at the box, knowing well what it contained, and knowing equally well the reason for that. *"I, too, have an ambition,"* the king had once told me. And that ambition had been to fulfill his vow to lead a crusade to the Holy Land. But Edward of England had done his best to thwart that ambition. Edward, even after suffering that terrible defeat

236

at Bannockburn, had refused to sign a peace treaty. Edward, indeed, had repeatedly threatened us with yet more invasions—thus forcing the king into the continued fighting needed to maintain the freedom won there.

For all of the fourteen years until that treaty was at last signed, in fact, the Bruce had continued to observe his own watchword of putting duty before ambition—but only to be struck then by the illness that had killed him. And now, in this little silver box was all that remained of him—his heart, that he had asked the Douglas to have embalmed and then carried at the forefront of that crusade.

"My dear and special friend . . ." Once again, in my mind, I heard his dying words to the Douglas—the words that all of us standing around then had wept to hear. *". . . since my body cannot go to achieve what my heart desires, I will send the heart instead of the body to accomplish my vow. And since I know not in all my realm of any knight more valiant, I require of you that you will take on this voyage for love of me, and to acquit my soul before God."*

With one hand reaching out to hover over the box, yet still not daring to touch it, I said to Sean:

"You went with the Douglas. You were one of his chosen band. Tell me. Tell me what happened."

Sean told me—not in his usual blustering style, but soberly, and in only a few words.

"We were passing through Spain," he said, "on our way to Jerusalem. The King of Spain enlisted the help of the Douglas against the Saracens who had occupied Granada.

237

The Douglas led the charge into battle, expecting the Spanish forces to follow on. But they did not. The Douglas saw himself about to be overwhelmed. He drew out from his doublet the box holding the Bruce's heart. He threw it far ahead of himself, crying out at the same time, *'Go first, brave heart, as you were ever wont to do.'* Then he set spurs to his horse, and followed after. When the field was clear again, I found the box under his dead body."

My hand came reverently to rest, at last, on the box. "And I will do with it now," I said, "what Lord Randolph so evidently expected of me. I will have it buried here, with all the honor that is its due."

We sat in silence then, with Sean's mind maybe crowded as much as mine was by thoughts of his time with the Bruce, and it was not till after a while that I asked, "Sean, you remember, do you not, how we prayed before that Battle of Bannockburn?"

"I remember." Soberly Sean answered. "I remember, too, the shiver that went up my back at the sound of all those other voices around me then."

"It was at the Borestone that I knelt," I told him. "I could see from there how the English king was watching the army at prayer. And, as I have learned since, his response was to cry out, *'Look, they kneel to beg for mercy.'* But some of those around him knew the feeling of our army better than he did, and it was one of these wiser men who told that king, *'Yes— but not of you. These men will conquer or die.'"*

"Aye." Sean sighed. "That was the spirit the Bruce put

into us every time we fought—but never more so than then!"

He rose on this, to take his leave. His bearing, I saw, was as soldierly as ever—but what would he do now with the country at peace and no more need for fighting spirits such as his? I made bold to ask him, and laughing a little, he told me:

"Settle down, of course. I have been given a grant of land for my services. I'll find a wife, settle there, and have children. Lads as cocky as myself, girls as strong and gentle as our Morag. All of them growing up free, too, in a free land. And that's no bad prospect, is it?"

"I'll christen them for you," I told him.

We shook hands on that to make a firm bargain of it before we finally parted, and I was left to consider what I might say at the burial service for the heart of the Bruce. With the silver box in my hand, then, I wandered over to the window of my study, my mind once again crowding with thoughts of him.

That time I took leave of him after the Battle of Bannockburn—he had not been rejoicing over his great victory. Instead, it had been in the chapel of Stirling Castle that I had found him, mourning the death of the English as well as the Scottish knights who had fallen in battle and had been brought to rest there.

I had knelt with him awhile, I remembered, beside the body of young Sir Walter of Ross. When we rose at last, I also remembered, he had seemed as sad to part with me as I was most certainly sad to part with him. And now there would be this most final of partings—the burial of his heart.

I had told Sean, too, that this burial would be carried out with all due honor. Yet what could I say there that had not already been said when his body had been laid in Dunfermline Abbey beside those of all our other Scottish kings? How otherwise could I honor him than with all the pomp and ceremony there had been then?

I sighed, turning away from the window with my mind roving back through all the years of his reign as King of Scots. The light from the window caught the colors of the illuminated text on my study wall—a text of only a few lines, but still precisely what was needed to stop my roving mind abruptly at one particular point in that reign.

The year of Our Lord thirteen hundred and twenty, six years after Bannockburn, yet still with Edward of England threatening to enforce his claim that Scotland was no more than just a part of the land that *he* ruled; thirteen hundred and twenty, when the king had called a parliament at Arbroath, and that parliament had published to the world a declaration that, far from this being so, Scotland was, and always would be, a free and independent kingdom.

The text on my study wall—I had taken the words of it from that Declaration of Independence. I had chosen these words, also, because none could have better conveyed the spirit the Bruce had infused into our whole nation. And there they were before me now, gleaming in all the heraldic brilliance of the gold and blue and green and red I had used to illuminate them.

So long as even only a hundred of us are left alive, we
shall never submit to the domination of the English. . . .

I spoke the first of these words aloud, hearing in them the
very voice of the Bruce himself—the voice that, like a trumpet, had so often called us into battle. And instantly, then, I
knew beyond doubt that the most fitting of all ways in which
I could honor him was to declaim this and all that followed
from it at the very moment when I lowered his heart into its
last resting place.

When I did so, also, I vowed, it would not be as the grave
and reverend Abbot of Melrose. Instead, it would be once
again as the king's swift rider announcing this last and also
the most lasting of all the messages he had entrusted to me.
And with all the pride I had ever felt in that role surging back
into me, I held even more closely to the little silver box that
contained his heart.

I heard the ring of the bell that announced the service of
Compline. Yet still, instead of hurrying to the chapel, I continued to stand there, the heart of Bruce pressed to my own
heart, and blazing brilliantly in my mind the rest of those
words that, throughout the long years of struggle, had been
the sum of the inspiration he had given to us all:

> For it is not for honor or glory or riches
> that we fight, but for freedom only,
> which no good man surrenders
> but with his life.

241

MOLLIE HUNTER

Hailed as "Scotland's most gifted storyteller" and currently living in Inverness, Mollie Hunter has drawn many award-winning novels from her country's history. They include You Never Knew Her As I Did, *a riveting tale about Mary, Queen of Scots, and her Carnegie Medal winner,* The Stronghold. A Sound of Chariots, *her autobiographical novel, won the 1991 Phoenix Award from the Children's Literature Association.*